"We cannot ignore what happened between us."

Theresa could barely look at him. "That was forever ago," she said, unconvincingly.

"And you think it wouldn't happen again?"

Her eyes flew to his face. Alexandros moved closer, his face a mask of grim determination, and her pulse went into overdrive. "I know it wouldn't," she whispered, remembering with a shiver how total his rejection of her had been. "One time with you was more than enough."

"Careful, *agape*. That sounds like a challenge."

Her knees knocked together, unsteady and weak.

"And the problem is, even when I know you are off-limits, or should be, I find myself intrigued by that challenge, desperate to make you eat your words." He lifted a finger to her chin, holding her face toward his so that every husky, warm breath she expelled brushed his lips like a caress. "Do you remember what it was like with us?"

"I remember everything about that night," she whispered.

"There is too much passion to ignore. I won't marry you unless you accept the inevitable— otherwise, we will both be in a hell of our own making."

Clare Connelly was raised in small-town Australia among a family of avid readers. She spent much of her childhood up a tree, Harlequin book in hand. Clare is married to her own real-life hero, and they live in a bungalow near the sea with their two children. She is frequently found staring into space—a surefire sign she is in the world of her characters. She has a penchant for French food and ice-cold champagne, and Harlequin novels continue to be her favorite-ever books. Writing for Harlequin Presents is a long-held dream. Clare can be contacted via clareconnelly.com or on her Facebook page.

Books by Clare Connelly

Harlequin Presents

My Forbidden Royal Fling
Crowned for His Desert Twins

Passionately Ever After...

Cinderella in the Billionaire's Castle

Signed, Sealed...Seduced

Cinderella's Night in Venice

The Cinderella Sisters

Vows on the Virgin's Terms
Forbidden Nights in Barcelona

Visit the Author Profile page
at Harlequin.com for more titles.

Clare Connelly

EMERGENCY MARRIAGE TO THE GREEK

HARLEQUIN
PRESENTS

**HARLEQUIN®
PRESENTS™**

Recycling programs
for this product may
not exist in your area.

ISBN-13: 978-1-335-73863-9

Emergency Marriage to the Greek

Copyright © 2022 by Clare Connelly

For questions and comments about the quality of this book,
please contact us at CustomerService@Harlequin.com.

Harlequin Enterprises ULC
22 Adelaide St. West, 41st Floor
Toronto, Ontario M5H 4E3, Canada
www.Harlequin.com

Printed in U.S.A.

EMERGENCY MARRIAGE
TO THE GREEK

PROLOGUE

POWERFUL, STRONG, SELF-MADE. Alexandros Zacharidis didn't make mistakes, but this was one of the biggest of his life.

He pulled away from her in shock, a thousand emotions possessing him, most keenly, betrayal and shock.

'Cristos.'

Theresa stared up at him, all wide, amber eyes, innocent pink cheeks, passion-swollen lips.

'Alex?' She frowned, her confusion obvious. That only angered him more. How could she not understand what he was feeling? 'What is it?'

Dumbfounded, he stared back, hands on hips, magnificent naked body on display, so her blush grew darker. 'This should not have happened.'

Her lips tugged downwards, lips that had been dragging across his torso minutes earlier, lower, sensually tasting him, flicking…

He groaned softly. 'It was a mistake.'

'I don't understand.' She sat up straighter. 'What's the matter?'

'You were a virgin.' The words were hissed between his teeth, his eyes barely able to hold hers. It was bad enough that he'd slept with his best friend's much younger sister, worse that he'd been her first, and unforgivable that it had happened on the day of Stavros's burial. He cursed in his mind, every curse he could think of, while waiting for her to respond.

Her eyes dipped down, not meeting his, and he felt a rush of frustration.

This shouldn't have happened, but it wasn't her fault. At least, it wasn't *only* her fault. He'd approached her, drawn her into an embrace, held her close until sympathy and grief had turned into something else, a low beating drum that had pulled at them both.

'You should have told me.'

'I—it didn't occur to me.' The words were heavy, uneven, as though she was fighting off tears. He needed to stop, to pull back, to let this go, but hell, he didn't like being surprised, he didn't like making mistakes. This was his worst nightmare.

'Dammit, Theresa. What were you thinking, coming here with me? You know who I am, *what* I am. Why would you do this?'

'I—thought—' Her skin was pale now, whiter than paper, as she looked around the room, as if for the answers she couldn't provide.

'I asked you to my room. I thought my meaning was clear. Did you come here expecting to have sex with me?'

The brutal directness of the question should have stopped him in his tracks, but nothing could. He wanted answers; he needed to understand this.

'*Cristos*, I need to know.' He stared at her until she nodded slowly, eyes haunted.

'Yes.'

'Why in God's name would you do that? You were a *virgin*. Did you think I would welcome this "gift"? Damn it, Theresa, you should have told me you were a virgin. I'm not interested in being your first. Do you understand what this was?'

Her lips parted and now her head moved side to side, her dark, glossy hair tumbling over her shoulders. Loyalty to Stavros should have held him silent, but Alex was blinded by emotion, shock at what he'd just allowed to happen overtaking all else.

'Sex. Just sex, something I do with women all the time, and it means nothing. Nothing. You're just a child, for God's sake.'

She flinched, and again he told himself to stop, to pull back, but an anger was rushing through his veins that he'd never known before. Loyalty was something Alex considered to be an unwavering trait, and his loyalty to Stavros was second to none. His best friend's body wasn't cold in the ground and Alex had seduced his sister?

He turned his back, stalking across the room and staring at the wall, panic rising inside of him, and a strange feeling that he might vomit.

'Get dressed, Theresa. You need to leave now.'

He left the room without a backwards glance, ashamed in a way he'd never forget for what he'd just allowed to happen. He swore that for as long as he lived he'd never think of her again, nor the weakness that had brought him to his knees.

A month after their night together, Theresa heard from Alex. It was unexpected, and completely unsettling. His voice at the other end of the line was business-like. None of the passion they'd shared that night came through in his call, nor did the white-hot anger he'd expressed afterwards.

'How are you?'

Her heart was about to explode out of her chest. Was that what he meant? 'Alex? Why are you calling me?'

'We slept together a month ago.'

Her pulse gushed. 'And?' The word was a thready whisper.

'If there were any consequences from that night—'

The purpose for his call then became crystal clear. She closed her eyes and shook her head. 'There weren't.'

A pause crackled down the phone line and then a rumbling noise. 'I'm glad. Then it's over.'

Bitterness filled her throat. 'Was it really so awful?'

She waited, the silence pulsing between them. 'Yes, *agape*. It really was.'

He disconnected the call and Theresa was glad they'd had this conversation over the phone, because that way he didn't get to see the tears sparkling in her eyes. She stared across the room, resolve hardening in the pit of her stomach.

Stavros's death had pulled her apart, and the night with Alex had added to that, but she refused to be a victim. She refused to let her parents continue to treat her like a baby. This was her life, and she had to live it, she had to reach out for what she wanted with both hands—and what she wanted, more than anything, was to forget Alexandros existed. To forget the perfection of his hands on her body, to erase him completely from her mind and life.

Stubbornness ran through her veins, and in that moment she was glad. She'd never think of him again.

CHAPTER ONE

TESSA STILL FOUND it hard to get used to the sight of her empty ring finger, despite the fact it was twelve months since her divorce had been finalised—thank goodness, because if she'd had to spend another day legally bound to the awful man she'd foolishly married, she feared she might have curled up into a ball and never unfurled again. None the less, she stared reflectively at the empty digit as the lift sailed higher and higher, towards the top of the Athens high-rise, telling herself the butterflies in her tummy had more to do with the rapid ascent than they did the fact she was about to come face-to-face with Alexandros Zacharidis for the first time in four years—and definitely not because of the proposal she was about to make.

After all, when it boiled down to it, her proposition was practically business, and that was a language the great Alexandros Zacharidis spoke fluently. Absentmindedly, she scratched off a speck of white paint from her knuckle—courtesy of the landscape she'd been working on that morning, whilst trying to steel herself to this.

What if she couldn't get through to him? That night they'd spent together had changed the shape of her universe. Not just because he'd been her first lover, and not because it had been right after losing her beloved brother—and Alex's best friend—but because the girlhood crush she'd nurtured for Alex for as long as she could remember had threatened to explode into something else entirely.

Until reality had intervened, and he'd pushed her away so hard and so fast she was still suffering whiplash.

Her heart had been broken. Or, at the time, she'd thought it was. She was too grown-up to believe in hearts and love and shattered dreams now. A lot had changed for her since that night, her idealism included.

The doors to the lift swished open, parting to reveal a floor of polished concrete with industrial pendant lights and a desk in the centre of the cavernous space that housed three receptionists. Behind them, a stunning view of the city was framed, like a painting—but Tessa fought her artist's natural inclination to study it in detail, steeling herself to focus on the task at hand.

'Hello,' she murmured, just a little unsteadily. 'Is Mr Zacharidis in?'

The receptionist nearest to Tessa frowned, scanning her computer screen. 'Good afternoon. Do you have an appointment?'

'No.'

'Ah.' The receptionist's brows beetled. 'I'm sorry, ma'am, but Mr Zacharidis has a very busy schedule.

If you'd like, I can check if he might be able to see you next week.'

But this morning's headlines were still swimming in her brain and Tessa knew this couldn't wait another day. Her father's health was fragile and worsening by the day. If her awful ex-husband kept selling stories to the tabloids, she worried about how that would affect her dad.

It wasn't in Tessa's nature to be bullish, so it was a sign of her desperation that she persisted. 'I really believe he'll make time for me.' Having attended an exclusive British boarding school, her accent was as crisp as the Queen's, and it gave the receptionist a moment's pause.

Tessa capitalised on her silence. 'Please,' she leaned forward, 'tell him I'm here.'

The receptionist's reluctance was obvious.

'My name is Tessa Anastakos.'

'Tessa Anastakos,' the receptionist repeated, as though trying to place her, and then jackknifing out of her chair as the penny dropped. After all, the Anastakos name was well-known not just in Athens, but throughout the world. 'Yes, ma'am.' She moved with elegant grace despite the fact she was almost running, towards a timber door across the foyer.

Tessa waited, and a moment later the receptionist reappeared. 'You were right.' She nodded crisply. 'Mr Zacharidis will see you now.'

'Thank you.' Despite her outward calm, the butterflies multiplied in her belly, so she felt a thousand and one things as she moved towards the door. Four years ago, grief had brought Alex and Tessa together, and in that perfect, magical moment she'd felt, briefly, healed, her grief salved, until he'd jerked away from her, obviously disgusted by what had happened. Her virginity had surprised him, but it was more than that. She was Stavros's younger sister, just a girl to him, as he'd callously pointed out whilst dressing as swiftly as he could.

Would he be any less disgusted by her proposal? Would his loyalty to her family mean he'd put aside his own personal feelings and agree to her plan? Uncertainty made her gut twist, so she pushed the doubts from her mind. If this was going to work, she had to think positively.

In preparation for this meeting, Tessa had written a thousand lists, each of them enumerating the reasons this made sense. What she hadn't done was Google Alexandros recently, so the moment the door opened and he turned to face her, she felt as though she'd been rammed by a cement truck.

Holy crap.

Her knees turned to jelly and her stomach swished and swooshed, but outwardly she remained business-like, her features barely shifting beyond the hint of a tight smile, even as memories of that night rocked her to the core.

'Damn it, Theresa, you should have told me you were a virgin. I'm not interested in being your first. Do you understand what this was?'

He'd gripped her upper arms, staring into her eyes, as if to make her understand better.

'*Sex. Just sex, something I do with women all the time, and it means nothing. Nothing. You're just a child, for God's sake.*'

She flinched at the recollection, his words as clear now as they had been on that awful night. He'd been wrong, in any event. At twenty-two, she might have been sheltered and innocent, but she was no longer a child, and she had been so sick of everyone perceiving her thus.

'Theresa.' He used the full version of her name, just as her brother always had, and something in the region of her heart panged.

'Everyone calls me Tessa.' She waved a hand through the air, her bare finger again catching her eye. 'How are you, Alex?'

The mockery in his expression was unmistakable, so for a moment her step faltered, and then, when his eyes dropped from her face to her breasts, and lower, to the sweep of her hips and back up again, she almost fell over. His inspection was slow and purposeful, setting little fires going beneath her skin.

'I'm very well, thank you, Theresa.' He said her name with a whisper of cynicism and her pulse picked up a notch. Had this been a gigantic mistake? He was teasing her, laughing at her, and Tessa really wasn't in the mood for it. All of Europe was already laughing at her after Jonathan's latest tabloid splash.

She jerked to a stop, tension radiating from the lines of her body. 'If you're going to treat me like a joke, I might as well turn around and leave.'

His eyes narrowed, fixed on her face, so her heart

almost stammered to a stop. He wore a navy-blue suit that had clearly been made for him, lovingly hand-stitched for his six-and-a-half-foot frame, his broad shoulders and muscular abdomen. The jacket was discarded on his chair back, and his crisp white shirt was unbuttoned at the neck to reveal the thick, tanned column of his neck. Memories of scraping her lips across his stubbled throat burst into her mind, unwelcome and surprising. Her pulse shifted into tsunami territory.

But it was his face that made everything go wonky.

When they'd slept together, she'd been twenty-two and innocent, completely sheltered from the world by over-protective parents; she'd had no idea about men and sex, despite the fact she'd attended school in her mother's native England, and college in New York. Now she was older, wiser. She'd been married, for goodness' sake, and her girlhood crush on Alex was eons ago, so her body's reaction was as unexpected as it was unwelcome.

She'd always been fascinated by the hundreds of little micro muscles of his face that moved when he felt something, the way his dark brown eyes turned an almost grey when he was angry, or gold when he laughed. And in the heat of passion his eyes closed, those long lashes fanned over his tanned cheeks, and his lips parted…

'Maybe this was a mistake.' The last couple of years had taken their toll on Tessa. She was emotionally bruised and battered and, despite the fact she was making her last stand here and now, she wasn't sure she was ready for what she'd feel if he rejected her. Or accepted!

She stood completely still as his eyes roamed her face, tracking all the changes he'd no doubt see there, boring into her caramel eyes and full red lips, dropping to her bare decolletage and the swell of her breasts, the nip of her waist and the slimness of her hips, right the way to the red-soled shoes she'd donned for confidence that morning, before returning, slowly, all the way back to her eyes. Heat followed his gaze, burning her with its intensity.

'Why don't you tell me what you came here for?' He crossed his arms over his broad chest, drawing her attention to the muscular definition there.

'I...' Uncharacteristically, she was lost for words. She swallowed, attempting to focus.

'It's been four years,' he pointed out with cool disinterest. 'Is this a social call? Or did you come here with something specific to discuss?'

Come on, tear off the Band-Aid!

'The latter,' she assured him, her voice cool as she strode towards the seats, conscious of the way his eyes followed her the entire way. She sat, crossing her legs neatly and keeping her hands clasped in her lap.

'Then by all means, enlighten me.' He was still pushing her away, just as he had that night, holding her at arm's length, so her stomach tightened and she doubted, again, the wisdom of this plan. But the purpose was clear: for her father, and the legacy he'd spent a lifetime building, she'd do whatever was necessary.

'I have a proposition for you,' she said haltingly.

'One that's going to sound completely crazy, admittedly. Hear me out?'

He dipped his head in acknowledgement, so she fumbled her fingers a bit, aware that she couldn't prevaricate for much longer.

'Naturally, whatever I say in here is confidential.'

'Of course.'

She offered him an apologetic grimace. After all, she had no reason to mistrust Alex, but after what she'd been through with her ex-husband, she couldn't help making the stipulation.

'I have to be sure,' she muttered.

His eyes were mocking. 'Cross my heart, hope to die.'

She ignored the droll sarcasm.

'I'm serious, Alex. This is—important.'

He dipped his head, silently encouraging her to continue.

'Okay.' Her voice shook a little. She swallowed, trying to clear her throat. 'You obviously know how my parents feel about you.'

He furrowed his brow. 'Is something the matter with Elizabeth and Orion?'

Grief was like a knife in her gut. She'd already lost so much, the idea of life without her father made her uncertain and cold to the bone. 'Dad's heart condition isn't responding to medication, and another surgery—while necessary—is not without risks.' She swallowed, desperate to keep her voice level even as grief saturated the words. 'Until he can have the procedure, his specialist has instructed him to avoid all stress.'

'I know he takes his health seriously,' Alex murmured, but there was tension in his voice too, that spoke volumes for how much he cared about her parents.

'They've always adored you,' she said softly, so he took a step closer, to hear her better, and she caught a hint of his masculine fragrance. Her stomach somersaulted. 'After Stavros died, they took a lot of comfort from how often you'd call in to see them.'

He said nothing, and that silence was powerfully unnerving.

'You're a connection to him,' she continued nervously, turning her honey-coloured eyes on the view of Athens without really seeing it. 'They love you.'

'Your parents are special people.'

She lifted a hand, drumming her fingers against the base of her throat. 'Yes, they are.' She forced her eyes back to his, knowing that if this was going to work, she'd have to appeal to his affection for them.

'They always hoped we would get together,' she blurted out, finding it hard to hold his gaze but knowing it was important. 'But I was never a big fan of the idea of an arranged marriage,' she said with a self-mocking grimace.

'Particularly not with me?' he drawled, and she held her breath, something in the region of her heart flickering as remembered girlhood wishes crashed right into her, when dreams of a big wedding to Alex had dominated all her thoughts. But she'd tried marriage once—it had been a disaster.

Straightening her spine, she shook her head once.

'No.' She bit down into her lower lip, a sense of ambivalence gripping her. 'You were always Stavros's friend, not mine.'

'Except for that one night.'

Her eyes swept shut, her throat thickening so swallowing was almost impossible. 'That night didn't make us friends.'

She didn't see the way his eyes combed her face with speculative appraisal, or her heart might have leaped right out of her chest.

'Why have you come here today?'

Nerves were a writhing pit of snakes in Tessa's belly. 'I'm worried about him.'

'Who?'

'Dad.' She blinked over at Alex, and her gut twisted for the genuine concern she saw, briefly, before he concealed it behind his usual mask of determination.

'Tell me what's going on.'

'I'm—' her mouth parted, then her lips pressed together. The words lodged hard in her jaw.

'Go on.' His command pulled at her, and she realised she didn't have anyone she could talk to about this. Jonathan had made her wary; his constant gossiping to tabloids had her on a knife's edge, terrified to trust anyone. But Alex was different—he always had been.

'He's really sick, Alex. I don't know when you last saw him—'

'Not for several months.'

Was that guilt in his voice?

'Then you won't have noticed. He's lost weight. He's tired, all the time. It's so unlike him.' Her voice cracked as she forced herself to admit what she'd known for some time. 'I don't think he has long.' The words were whispered.

Alex's frown was contemplative. 'You think? Or you know?'

Her eyes met his and her lower lip trembled. 'I know,' she whispered, standing then, moving to the window on knees that were unsteady. 'It's nothing he's said, but I can just tell. He keeps talking about Mum, about how to take care of her.' She lifted a finger and dashed at a tear before it could spill over. She'd told herself she wouldn't do this! Not here, and not in front of this man; not after how he'd treated her.

Her nerves pulled taut. 'If there was anyone else I could ask…' she said slowly. 'You have to understand, I've looked at this from every angle.'

'You need help with your father?'

'No…yes.' She sighed with exasperation. 'In a sense, yes. I…made a mistake, Alex, and I need help to fix it.'

'You're not making sense.'

'I know.' She rubbed her temples. 'My parents always hated him.'

'Who?'

'My ex-husband, Jonathan.' She couldn't meet his eyes. So much of her choice to marry Jonathan was bound up in Alex's cold-hearted rejection of her. Her entire world had then been tipped on its edge—by the death of Stavros, by sleeping with Alex and the way he'd reacted, by her parents' total and all-consuming sense of grief, which had translated into an over-protectiveness that was beyond suffocating. Jonathan had been her way out, she just hadn't realised she was jumping out of the frying pan into the fire.

'So, he is your ex-husband now. Doesn't that solve the problem?'

'If only it were that simple. Unfortunately, he's taken to blathering about our marriage to anyone who'll listen. As I speak, he's locked away for *Celebrity Housemate*—you know, that fly-on-the-wall reality show?—and the promotional clips they're airing are all about me.'

His silence wasn't particularly encouraging.

'Every time there's an article maligning me, or our family, it affects Dad. I need it to stop.'

'Yes,' he agreed, arms crossed over his chest again. 'I can see that. Would you like me to speak to my lawyers?'

'That won't work.' She shook her head. 'I've tried it. He won't sign an NDA, as it's far more profitable to sing like a canary.'

'He's significantly underestimating your net worth, then.'

'He's trying to parlay our marriage into lasting fame and fortune.' She rolled her eyes. 'It's not his fault. He had nothing, and he doesn't want to go back to that.'

'Was the divorce settlement not generous enough?'

'I don't think it would have mattered what I gave him; he'd have always wanted more.'

Disapproval curved Alex's symmetrical lips. 'He sounds like a catch.'

He was only echoing her own thoughts, but she

wasn't in the mood to be spoken down to. 'I didn't come here to appraise my husband's shortcomings.'

'Ex-husband,' he corrected factually. 'And apparently, you came here because you need my help. Tell me how.'

'I want to take back control,' she said with a small jut of her chin, quiet determination steadying the words. 'Part of the reason he's been able to blather on in the press is because I completely withdrew.'

Alex's eyes were heavy on her face, but she didn't look directly at him.

'Why? What have you been doing?'

Great question, without an answer. Her art had largely stalled, as stress about her father, her marriage, her mother, had all bundled together to paralyse her creativity. 'I never expected to get divorced,' she murmured, 'then again, I never expected to be married to someone like him.'

A sharp exhalation drew her eyes to Alex's face. 'What does that mean?'

She shook her head, lost for words.

'It doesn't matter.' The awful truth of her marriage was something she needed to hold close.

Alex tensed. 'Did he hurt you?'

Theresa shook her head. 'He didn't hit me,' she whispered, eyes moist. 'But he hurt me in other ways.' Her eyes hid from him. 'He was controlling. Angry. Jealous. Possessive. And when he felt that I wasn't paying him enough attention, he sought to destroy my confidence. He insulted me, always. Sometimes subtly, sometimes not. Sometimes privately, sometimes not. It's amazing how quickly a person can break you down, and make you lose all faith in your own abilities. And when he didn't get what he wanted, he went out and slept with someone else, then made sure I heard all about it.' Bitterness flooded her words.

'And yet you stayed with him?'

How could she explain to Alex? Her marriage had been untenable after only a few months, but Jonathan had too much over her, and the idea of divorcing him, of upsetting her parents, had kept her right where she was.

'He always threatened to do this, if I left him,' she said with soft resignation. 'I didn't want this to be my life, my parents' life, and so I stayed with him until I really couldn't bear it any longer.'

'You should have given him nothing in the divorce,' he spat angrily.

'In the end, I just wanted him to go away.' Her eyes were haunted.

'No wonder your parents hate him.'

She nodded awkwardly. 'I have put them through hell, Alex.'

'It sounds to me as though you are the one who's been through hell.'

Sympathy would be her undoing. She focused on her parents rather than allowing his words to serve as any kind of balm. 'It's been hard on them, and after Stavros, it's the last thing they need. Now, with Dad's health, I need to make everything right. I need to fix this.'

'And you have a plan?'

'Yes, that's exactly right.' She swallowed past the

tangle of nerves. 'I can see a solution to everything, but I have no idea if you'll agree. It's actually going to sound very mad, I'm afraid, but there's nothing for it. No idea's too crazy, right?'

He didn't look convinced. 'Go on.'

Her stomach squeezed. *Do it.* Get it over with. 'I was wondering how you'd feel about marrying me, Alex?'

The sound of a pin dropping would have echoed through the silent room.

'Just to be clear—is this a joke?'

'No.' Her pretty lips formed a perfect Cupid's bow as she grimaced, and her eyes skittered away from him, as they'd done far too frequently during this short meeting.

He couldn't say what he'd been expecting, but definitely not this.

'So you came to my office to propose?' he demanded, wondering at the anger that was sparking low down in his gut. He hadn't seen Theresa Anastakos in years—she shouldn't still be able to invoke this kind of response in him—but there was no questioning the fact that she'd shot his senses into overdrive from the moment of her arrival, just as she had that night.

Sleeping with her had been a mistake he regretted to this day, almost as much as he did the cruel words he'd thrown at her afterwards. But the truth was, he'd have said anything in that moment to put a stop to what had happened. If he could have taken back that night, he would have. It had been madness. He still wasn't over it. Not the sex, but the fact he'd made a mistake by sleeping with her at all, and Alex didn't *make* mistakes.

Yet the desire he felt for her was unmistakable. Even now, after living with the guilt of his betrayal of Stavros, he couldn't look at Theresa without those old feelings stirring, as potently demanding as ever. But Theresa was not a mistake he intended to make twice, no matter how tempted he was.

'I know it sounds mad,' she admitted.

'Mad? It's worse than that. It's impossible.'

Her skin paled to the colour of cream. 'Why?'

'Because—' He cursed softly. 'You may not have realised this about me, but I'm hardly the marrying kind.'

'My parents think you are.'

'Your parents are far too generous in their assessment. Believe me, I could never make you happy.'

'I'm not looking for you to make me happy,' she volleyed back with urgency. 'I've already been married once and I think the whole idea stinks.'

'On this, we are in agreement.'

Her eyes met his, a challenge in their depths, so a strange tightening gripped his gut. He stood perfectly still, refusing to be moved by her request.

'You're a businessman, and I'm suggesting a businesslike marriage. We'll sign some contracts, pose for a few photos, then move on with our lives.'

He shook his head in a demurral. 'I can see why you're suggesting this, but what is in it for me?' Her cheeks flushed and an answering awareness flared to life inside of him, so danger sirens blared continually. 'A businesslike arrangement would involve us both getting something we wanted from the deal,' he continued, careful not to betray the direction of his thoughts. 'What do I get out of it?'

'Apart from making a man you purport to care about happy?'

'I care for and respect your parents, but I am too old to do anything for anyone else. What else have you got?'

She flinched, evidently not expecting this barrier. 'Tell me what you'd want.'

'Nothing,' he was quick to respond, even as his whole body tightened with a surge of powerful attraction, a need to possess her that was every bit as strong as it had been four years earlier. He closed his eyes against its power and sway, but that was worse, because his mind homed in on another point in the marriage's favour, something he could present as a term of his own.

'There must be something,' she pleaded now, sucking in a sharp breath, and her breasts thrust forward, so for a brief moment he was powerless to resist and allowed his gaze to drop, to admire the sweet swell of her cleavage against the pale dress she wore, awareness of her femininity stirring something to life inside of him.

The night they'd made love, they hadn't been Alex and Tessa. They'd been as wild as animals, driven by primal grief, so he'd torn her clothes from her body and she'd scratched his back and they'd bitten one another and made love so hard and fast that it hadn't been until he entered her that he realised it was her first time. And then it was too late, they were both too caught up in the moment, too desperate to feel the heavenly release to do anything but surrender to it completely. Everything about that night had been feral and elemental, had made perfect sense at the time, and none in the moments immediately afterwards, when he'd realised that he'd betrayed some vital bond of trust, crossing a line he should never have gone near.

'Please, Alex, won't you think about it?' For a moment, he was reminded of Stavros, and how he would do anything for his dear friend. Guilt chafed at him. He'd slept with Theresa. Didn't he have a moral obligation to help her in some way? Because of Stavros. Because of her parents. Because of how he'd treated her in the past.

And yet, the idea of marriage was anathema to him. It always had been.

'It would never be real,' he heard himself say, the acquiescence close to agreement, so her eyes widened with triumph.

'I don't want real.'

He swore under his breath, dragging a hand through his hair. 'I mean it, Theresa. If we were to do this, you would be nothing to me. The kid sister of a dear friend. Nothing more.'

Her eyes glinted with an emotion he didn't recognise, determination clamping her features into a mask of resolve. 'As always,' she said with a terse nod. 'So tell me what you need? What can I offer to get you to say yes?'

He was alone. Utterly and completely. His best friend had died—Stavros had been more like a brother to Alex, anyway. He was the only son of an only son. There were no siblings, aunts, uncles, cousins. There was no other Zacharidis in his life. That hadn't bothered him until his father's death, and then, the idea of being an island on his own, all his life, had made something shift in his gut. The pledge he'd made, decades earlier, to stay single and childless, to do whatever he could to avoid the hell of his parents' marriage and his own childhood, no longer seemed as important as a physical need to procreate, a biological urge to see a part of himself in the world, to know that he wasn't completely alone.

No one could have been more surprised by this urge than Alex, and perhaps he might have quelled it, or fought it, over time. But here was Tessa, offering him a marriage, asking him what he would want out of that marriage... Ever the opportunist—how else did a person build an empire like Alex's?—he saw a way to turn this to his advantage, and he shamelessly prepared to take it, even as regret was already promising to expand through him, even when he knew Stavros would hate him for this.

He straightened, crossing his arms over his broad chest, aware of the way her eyes soaked up the gesture, landing and remaining on his mid-section before she reluctantly lifted them back to his face.

'You might not like the conditions I'd have, if I were to agree to this.'

CHAPTER TWO

'IF' WAS WAY better than what she'd come here expecting. In her heart of hearts, she'd been almost certain that his answer would be no, so it was a sign of how desperate Tessa was that she'd even gone through with this.

'If' was the starting of a negotiation. Her insides squished with a mix of adrenaline and anxiety.

'I'd like to hear them,' she said unsteadily.

He took two steps towards her, closing the distance and knocking her nerves sideways. Her heart stammered inside her ribcage and despite the fact she wasn't an inexperienced, sheltered twenty-two-year-old any more, for a moment she sure felt like one.

She held her breath as he came to stand right in front of her, his alpine scent dangerously addictive, so she inhaled deeply before she could stop herself, tasting him at the back of her throat and wanting... Her eyes flared wide as she immediately tamped down on her illicit thoughts. This wouldn't work if she *wanted* him. Desire was a double-edged sword; she'd felt the sting of its blade before and would do whatever she could to avoid that.

'So?' she asked, the word emerging as a husky prompt.

His smile was slow to spread, and it made her tummy feel all hollowed out.

'Tell me about the kind of marriage you'd imagine us having.'

'That's a question, not a term.'

He dipped his head in agreement.

Rather than argue on a technicality, she acknowledged it was fair for him to want to understand exactly how this would work.

'We'd have to live together,' she said haltingly. 'At least initially. Thanks to Jonathan, there's a level of public scrutiny around my private life.' She couldn't contain a small shudder. 'Obviously, I'm hopeful that will die down. At some point, I would imagine we could go back to living almost completely independently.'

'I see.'

'It would really be a marriage in name only. We'd give the media a new angle, and hopefully Jonathan's relevance would fade into obscurity. But more than that, most importantly,' her voice trembled, 'Dad would have some peace of mind, at the end of his life.'

His obsidian eyes didn't move. If he was touched by concern for her father, he didn't show it. Such was the power of Alexandros Zacharidis. He was a skilled negotiator, an intimidating executive. 'And what if I told you I'd want more than that?' he asked, his eyes probing her, reading her, so she suspected he could see all her doubts and uncertainties, and so much more.

'Which brings us back to your terms,' she pointed out, huskily. 'Why don't you tell me what they are, so we can decide if this will work? I'm prepared to be flexible,' she added, after a beat.

His eyes were gently mocking, and her insides turned to goo.

'Am I to understand you're suggesting a marriage without intimacy?'

Heat scored her nerves even as painful memories of her own marriage turned her veins to ice. Her crisp nod was belied by her stuttering voice. 'Behind closed doors, we wouldn't need to pretend we were anything more than…polite acquaintances.'

'Is that what we are?' The words held a gruff challenge.

'We haven't seen each other in years,' she pointed out acerbically. 'I don't know if we could even say we're acquainted any more.'

'And yet you came to me and poured out your heart, begging me to help you.'

She swallowed, her throat scratchy and dry. 'Was that a mistake?'

'The mistake was in thinking the marriage you're suggesting would ever work.'

Her insides twisted and uncertainty lurched through her. 'Why wouldn't it?'

Another laugh, so soft it was as though it had been designed just for her ears, and his husky warmth floated across, teasing the sensitive skin of her neck.

'We cannot ignore what happened between us.' She could barely look at him.

'That was for ever ago,' she said, unconvincingly.

'And you think it wouldn't happen again?'

Her eyes flew to his face. He moved closer, his expression a mask of grim determination, and her pulse went into overdrive.

'I know it wouldn't,' she whispered, remembering with a shiver how total his rejection of her had been. The crush she'd harboured for him for so long, the desire he'd stirred in her, the culmination of her grief and need and wanting that had brought them together, and the way he'd dismissed her afterwards, showing her so clearly that she meant nothing to him. 'One time with you was more than enough.'

'Careful, *agape*. That sounds like a challenge.'

Her knees knocked together, unsteady and weak.

'And the problem is, even when I know you are off limits, or should be, I find myself intrigued by that challenge, desperate to make you eat your words.' He lifted a finger to her chin, holding her face towards his, so that every husky, warm breath she expelled brushed his lips like a caress. 'Do you remember what it was like with us?'

'I remember everything about that night,' she whispered, eyes sweeping shut to hide the hurt that was still layered over her heart.

'There is too much passion to ignore. I won't marry you unless you accept the inevitable—otherwise we will both be in a hell of our own making.'

She groaned, desperately tempted, and also terrified, because Jonathan had destroyed beyond repair every normal emotion and sense she possessed. She was too broken by his betrayal to even contemplate sleeping with Alex. 'How can you say that? You didn't want me four years ago, why do you think you're going to want me now?'

His eyes narrowed, his lips pursed tight as though he was physically restraining himself from speaking.

'I'm serious, Alex. What happened between us was a stupid mistake. We both regretted it,' she added, even when the words didn't ring true for Tessa. Not completely. 'Do you think anything is served by agreeing to sleep together again?'

'It was a mistake,' he agreed with a dip of his head. 'But that isn't to say it wasn't also enjoyable.'

She flinched. Jonathan's criticisms came barrelling towards her. She looked away, lips clamped tight.

'I was there, remember? You didn't seem like a man who enjoyed anything about what we did.'

His expression didn't change. 'I regretted sleeping with you because of who you are. It had nothing to do with the sex itself.'

'I thought it was "awful"?'

A frown gashed over his face. 'It was.'

Her laugh was a strangled sound. 'Lovely. Thanks for that.' Just what she needed!

'The *fact* we slept together was awful. You are Stavros's baby sister—how did you expect me to react?'

Her heart kicked up a notch as she contemplated that. For years she'd believed his insult had been a reflection on the experience, rather than the circumstances surrounding it. 'I betrayed him. How could I take pleasure in that?'

'And now?' she pushed. 'You don't seem to have that reservation any more.'

'You're wrong,' he responded, nostrils flaring as he expelled a sharp breath. 'But I am also a realist. If I marry you, it will be to help you, and your parents, and I have to believe Stavros would want me to do what I could. But there is no marriage if we cannot acknowledge that what drove us together that night still exists between us.'

Her lips parted as she searched for how to respond. That night was still a source of too much pain. She looked over his shoulder, stomach twisted into knots. 'Are you saying you'll marry me if I agree to sleep with you?'

'No.' The word was darkly uttered. 'I'm saying this marriage will only work if you admit sex is going to happen between us, whether that's convenient or not. I don't want to go through the emotional upheaval of having you come to terms with that side of our relationship once we are married. We are two consenting adults—if we choose to indulge our bodies' needs, then that's not a big deal. As with that night, it would mean nothing.'

She pulled away from him, her heart racing, because everything he'd said was anathema to her. Sex mattered. It had always mattered to Tessa. It was a large part of why her marriage had failed—how could she sleep with a man who treated her so badly? Whom she didn't love?

'Is there anything else?' she whispered, wrapping her arms around her body.

'Are you saying you accept what I have said?'

'I'm just getting a full picture of what you want before I decide,' she corrected unevenly, body already tingling at the prospect of his suggestion.

'There is one other thing.'

Slowly she looked at him, heart in her throat.

'My father died six months ago.'

She nodded. 'I heard. My mother mentioned…' She tapered off into nothing, unsure how to offer condolences.

'After he was buried, I stood in the middle of his empty home and I realised something I should have been prepared for.' He paused, not for effect, so much as to rally his thoughts. 'I was alone.' His eyes stared into the distance. 'I have no other family. No siblings, cousins, no one.'

She didn't know what to say, nor did she understand why he was telling her this.

'My parents destroyed any thoughts I might have had on marriage as a desirable objective in life. I don't see the point to it, frankly.' Curiosity sparked in her chest. She remembered throwaway comments her parents had made over the years about his family. She'd gathered that it had been quite a volatile relationship, but she didn't know any particulars. 'Standing there, completely alone, I had to contemplate what that meant. For six months, I have grappled with my isolation in this life. Largely, this has been by choice. I have avoided relationships assiduously.'

She remembered what that felt like. Being pushed away by Alex was an experience from which she doubted she'd ever really recover.

'But something strange has happened to me since my father's death.'

'Oh?' Unconsciously, she moved towards him, fascinated.

'I have a yearning not to be alone.'

She frowned. 'So you've changed your mind about marriage, then?'

He ignored that. 'I want children, Theresa. A family. I want to have descendants to pass on my wealth to. I want…' He stared at her, as if evaluating her for a moment before deciding he should proceed. 'I want my life to matter beyond the balance of my bank account.'

Sympathy flooded her, alongside compassion, and, more terrifyingly, adrenaline and excitement, for his list of demands was filling out something inside of her, something she'd denied for a long time, because Jonathan was far from a suitable man to have children with.

'Your life does matter. Of course it does. A child doesn't make you inherently more or less valuable.'

His eyes bored into hers. 'Believe me, this is the last thing I expected to find myself wanting.'

Tessa considered that a moment. 'So what were you planning to do about it?'

'Nothing, at this stage, perhaps ever.' He shrugged, his eyes narrowing contemplatively. 'And yet, here you are, offering yourself to me on a silver platter.'

'I wouldn't say that, exactly' came the breathy response. Because no matter what words she responded with, an image was blooming in her mind and she couldn't ignore the temptation of it.

'I will only agree to this marriage on two conditions. The first is that you acknowledge the full extent of what you're asking for. Sex between us is inevitable— but can you accept that? And do you understand that I mean sex without any emotional strings?'

She almost walked out on him then. Only the thought of her father's worsening health had her hold her ground.

'And the second is that you fully understand my desire for children. If you are not on the same page, this could never work.'

Her fingers trembled. Another speck of paint caught her eye, a vibrant purple thanks to the agapanthus hedge she'd been rendering to canvas hours earlier. She ran her finger over it carelessly. It was the duty of an artist to be paint splattered, and since her divorce she'd been trying to throw herself back into her art, indulging the work Jonathan had always sneered at as being 'beneath' her.

'I realise it's a curve ball.' He shrugged his broad shoulders, moving away from her a little. 'If the idea of this marriage no longer appeals to you, then you're free to leave. This conversation never happened.'

Her smile was hollow, her stomach in knots. 'It's not that simple,' she whispered, moving towards the window and pressing her over-warm forehead against the thickened glass. Her throat was dry and her head ached.

'My parents have lost so much. After Stavros, they've never been the same. I know I'm no substitute for him.'

'What does that mean?' His tone was sharp, his voice close. She didn't move. Grief was wrapping around her, as fresh now as it had been on that day so many years earlier.

'I'm not like them,' she whispered softly. 'My mum, dad, Stav. They're all cut from the same cloth. I'm a cuckoo in the nest, an enigma. They never got me. Marrying Jonathan was supposed to be—' She shook her head, not wanting to discuss her husband then, nor the reason she'd jumped far too rashly into the engagement. 'I didn't mean to compound their sadness, but I did. I've put them through the wringer, and I just want to give them this gift—I want to do something they'll be proud of, just once in my life, before it's too late. Dad—' Her voice shook but she pushed herself to standing, refusing to show any further signs of weakness to this man.

She turned to face him, so overwhelmed by the strength of her feelings that she didn't see the emotions in his eyes, the pity in the depth of his gaze. 'I'm sure they're proud of you.'

She brushed aside his meaningless reassurance. She knew her parents, and she knew how they felt about her. They loved her, they couldn't bear the thought of something happening to her, but they valued her as an object, rather than a person all of her own. Her interests, her passions, her art, they were meaningless to her family. But that didn't change the fact she'd do anything for her parents, for the father who was nearing the end of his life.

'Yes,' she whispered. 'Let's do this.' Before she let common sense return and she backed out of the scenario altogether.

His only response was a small shift of his head. 'Come to my house tonight.'

Her eyes flared wide. 'What? Why?'

His laugh was a hoarse sound that split her heart in two. 'To discuss the details, *agape*. Don't worry. I'll keep my hands to myself—unless you don't want me to?'

Heat flooded her cheeks. Was she so transparent? 'What details?'

'Where we'll live, for starters. When we'll marry. How we'll announce it and tell your parents. These things matter.'

He was right. There were logistics to plan for. Only everything felt all wobbly. She'd been so sure this would be a businesslike marriage proposal and he'd completely redefined the borders of those expectations. Not to mention, coming face to face with Alex for the first time in four years made it impossible to forget just how much she'd used to worship him. That crush had become a source of so much embarrassment, so it was shocking to discover that she still couldn't look at him without going weak at the knees.

She couldn't have a second disastrous marriage to her name. She had to be sure they would make a go of this—and his idea of discussing the details made sense.

This would work. It would be fine. 'Okay,' she said on a small exhalation. 'Tonight.'

He had expected her to refuse. He'd goaded her, challenged her, thinking she'd turn her back on this whole preposterous idea and walk away. And now that she'd accepted, he had to make his peace with it, because she was offering him something he hadn't even fully acknowledged to himself that he wanted.

'You understand the limits of this?' he pushed, just to be certain. She was Stavros's sister, and, while the lines were getting blurred, he could still control the boundaries of their relationship. He had a lifetime of experience with that, after all.

'Yes.' It was as though a switch had been flicked. Now that she'd accepted his terms, the uncertainty had disappeared, leaving determination in her beautiful face. And she *was* beautiful, he contemplated with a tightening in his groin. As beautiful now as she had been then, as she had been as a gawky, uncertain teenager and she'd smiled at him as though he was the centre of the universe.

Stavros had always been protective though. *'She's way too young for you. Don't even think about it.'* And she had been. Even the night they'd slept together, at twenty-two, she'd still been far too inexperienced and sheltered for a man like him—ten years older and far more worldly.

He'd used her.

She'd had a crush on him for years—he couldn't have missed the way she'd used to stare at him, and when she'd walked through the hotel bar, distracted and grieving, he'd moved to intercept her, drawing her into his arms because he'd needed the contact, the physical connection, the distraction.

The taste of acid filled his mouth.

He disgusted himself.

Stavros had only been buried hours earlier and there was Alex disregarding his friend's often stated warning, seducing his younger, innocent sister for his own selfish needs.

There had been other women in the bar that night, other women he could have turned to in order to slake his needs, and yet he'd chosen Tessa. He'd betrayed Stavros and Alex had never forgiven himself for that. He'd pledged he would never see Tessa again, that he'd never indulge that weakness, and he'd been right to avoid her. Only he thought of her often, not because of who she was, but because of the weakness she'd brought out in him, and how much he'd hated that. He should have turned her away the moment she'd arrived. He should have told his assistant to send her away. But he'd been curious, and wanting to see her, to see how she'd changed and grown.

Their marriage would be a gift to her parents, and so too would a child be. Surely even Stavros, then, would have approved of this? With a sound of frustration, he shook his head. There was no way his best friend would *ever* condone the marriage of Alex to Tessa. Stavros had always protected Tessa, and he knew, better than anyone, what demons pursued Alex. He knew about Alex's parents' marriage, the torment of living with a couple who could swing from wildly happy to murderously enraged in the blink of an eye, the torture of feeling that you were losing not one, but two parents every time they argued. The instability of growing up in a home split in half by emotional arguments, or vibrating with tension and silence. His parents had hated each other, but they'd hated the idea of separating even more, and so they'd stayed together, trapped in their loveless marriage, until they couldn't survive another day, and finally they had parted, both destroyed in every way that mattered by the torment they'd put one another through.

Alex had known he would never marry, from a young age, and he had told Stavros this on many occasions. Stavros had teased him, saying it was only because Alex liked to bed a different woman each night, that he might feel differently if he actually got to know one of the women he slept with. But Alex had been resolute. Sex was sex, he saw no purpose in getting to know the women he slept with—and there hadn't been any complaints from them, anyway.

But sleeping with Tessa had cheapened everything about his way of life. He'd been so angry with himself, and, unfairly, so angry with her, for being in the lobby, for walking past him, for looking at him as though he could fix everything, for understanding, as no one else could, what Stavros's death had cost Alex. Hell, he'd even been angry at her for being a virgin—a twenty-two-year-old virgin! He hadn't wanted that gift, the special uniqueness of what they'd shared. Betraying Stavros was bad enough, but being her first?

Goddammit.

They'd discussed a marriage without emotion, but Alex wasn't a fool. For Tessa had been the only woman who'd ever invoked anything close to sentiment in him—even if they had been dark emotions—and he would now have to spend a lifetime ensuring it never happened again. Feelings had no place in his marriage—they never would.

CHAPTER THREE

THE DRIVEWAY GATES opened as soon as she keyed in the security code he'd given her, and when she pulled up in front of the stunning house she noted the door was open. It was one of the best areas of Athens, and he clearly felt confident with the security arrangements in place. A quick study of the façade showed several discreet cameras, which she suspected held a live feed to some data cloud somewhere, if not a real-time monitoring service.

She stepped out of the car with innate elegance, smoothing a hand over her dress, wincing a little as the late-afternoon sun cut through her like a blade. She shielded her eyes, scanning the house with interest, noting the mid-century modern architecture that put her in mind of a Frank Lloyd Wright masterpiece, with carved balconies overlapping one another, part stone, part timber. The garden was breathtakingly lovely too. Formal and wild at the same time, the juxtaposition of conscious design elements was perfectly offset by rambling flowers and a canopy of trees that sheltered the drive. Grabbing her leather document wallet from the back seat, Tessa moved away from the car with an effort to keep her breathing steady.

She knew it might have seemed like overkill, but, having been married once before, Tessa could only go through with this if she knew she had complete control. It needed to be on her terms, and so she'd brought a sense of armour with her: a prenuptial agreement that would guarantee they could keep this marriage rational, despite the terms he'd stipulated.

This wasn't going to be anything like her marriage to Jonathan, she reminded herself, poking her head through the doorway and looking around. Besides a pair of polished brown shoes, there was no sign of Alex.

'Hello?' she called out, clearing her throat and trying again, louder this time.

There was no reply. Clutching her phone in one hand, she moved deeper into his home, the click-clacking of her sandals on the tiles making her feel reassured and in command.

If it was possible, the interior of his home exceeded the exterior. The mid-century modern features continued internally, with tall ceilings, timber beams and glass everywhere, as well as a sunken lounge conversation pit, grey carpets meeting slate floors and light fittings that were like something out of *The Jetsons*.

She wove past an Eames armchair, black leather with moulded walnut wood, and then, through large timber-framed glass sliding doors, onto a pool area that was perfectly placed to take advantage of the views of Athens. But apart from a brief glimpse of buildings and the most stunning late-evening sky she'd seen in a long time, Tessa wasn't capable of taking any further note of the details of his property, because Alexandros Zacharidis was swimming in said infinity pool, his powerful arms pulling him through the water as though swimming were as easy for him as walking was for her. Arms that had been shielded from her view that afternoon were now on full display, rippling, rounded biceps covered in rivulets of adoring water, glowing beneath the early evening sun, his skin golden—no, bronzed, like any of the sculptures of ancient Gods she'd admired at the museums. Her mouth was drier than the desert at full sun and her feet were planted to the ground, her heels no longer offering a reassuring clickety-clack as if they too were struck dumb by the sight of him like this.

As he reached the end of the pool he came to a halt, standing so his ridged pectoral muscles were on full display, his dark hair a pelt against his head until he shook it vigorously from one direction to the next, flicking droplets over the tiles, so Tessa instinctively stepped back rather than getting splashed. Her involuntary movement drew his attention and he turned to face her, a wolfish smile spreading slowly over his features.

'You came.' Was she imagining the mocking amusement beneath the benign words? Was she the only one who heard the double entendre?

He could have swum to the edge of the pool, where there was a perfectly good set of steps available, but instead Alex pulled himself out of the water right where he was, giving that magnificent body a chance to tighten as she watched, each muscle taut as he moved with easy athleticism from the water, towards a sun-bed that was perilously close to her. She took several more steps backwards, eyes on him warily, tongue too thick to enable her to speak, so she simply nodded as he approached, one hand gripping her briefcase more tightly, the other almost strangling her phone.

'I'm glad.' Up close, she could see the fascinating glitter of water droplets against his even more fasci-nating face.

Oh, good heavens.

This was, perhaps, her worst idea ever. How could she possibly have a businesslike marriage with some-one she was clearly still attracted to? What had she been thinking?

'Nice house,' she murmured, her voice strangled, as he reached for a towel and wrapped it around his neck. She tried, she really tried, to keep her eyes on his face, but standing there like that, dripping and ba-sically naked, how could she not look? Just quickly. Of its own volition, her gaze slipped lower, to his chest, lower still to his narrow hips, and disastrously to the black shorts which were clinging to him like a second skin. Their dark colour hid most of the detail but that didn't stop her cheeks from flaming red as memories of his possession steamed through her.

'Care to join me?' He gestured to the pool, so her attention jerked back to his face, and then beyond Alex to the turquoise water. Despite her being paralysed by the strength of her attraction, the pool was tempting. The afternoon had been hot, and the water looked so inviting. But was it the water, or the idea of being close to him, barely dressed, that had her desperate to accept his suggestion?

'No,' she said quickly, frowning as she returned her attention to his face. 'We had a meeting scheduled, didn't we?'

'We did,' he agreed, his expression giving nothing away. 'But I don't think we decided firmly on the venue.'

'Not the swimming pool,' she clarified.

'Right, because heaven forbid we have fun while we discuss—'

'This isn't fun for me,' she cut in quickly. 'In fact, it's something of an emergency.'

Speculation darkened his eyes and she swallowed, aware she was showing more than she wanted to, hating the panic that curdled her voice.

'Come inside then,' he invited with a firm nod, gesturing to the sliding glass doors.

'Thank you.' She followed behind him, aware she should have more willpower than to stare at his bottom as he walked ahead of her, turning left and moving into a large, open-plan kitchen. More architectural features drew her eyes here, and she tried to focus on them rather than Alex, because she needed the momentary reprieve.

'The house is beautiful,' she repeated.

'Yes.' He withdrew a bottle of champagne from the fridge, the famous label speaking immediately of exclusivity and expense, then filled two stemless glasses before retrieving a bowl of fruit—grapes, strawberries and peeled citrus—and placing it between them. 'Help yourself.' He gestured to the fruit. 'Give me a moment to get changed.'

'Fine.' The word couldn't have come across any more curtly, and she flinched inwardly. Why the hell was he agreeing to this? He could find any number of women to bear his children. But not without emotional complications, she reminded herself after a beat. Alex didn't want a 'real' marriage, any more than she did.

And what about having his child, or children? The idea sat in her throat like gravel. All afternoon, she'd gone over that requirement of his, remembering how sure she'd been, once upon a time, that she wanted children. But day after day of marriage to Jonathan had killed that dream for her, and Tessa wasn't sure she could revive it.

She placed her briefcase on one of the barstools and reached for the champagne, taking a single sip before replacing the glass on the counter.

He returned quickly enough, dressed—thankfully— in a pair of khaki shorts and a white T-shirt, so all she had to contend with was the fascinating spectre of his tanned legs with muscular calves and the perfect covering of dark hair. So masculine and...inwardly she groaned. This was going to be a disaster.

'Okay.' He took up a matching position to hers, bracing his palms on either side of the counter, watching her with a small flicker of amusement at the corner of his lips. 'Let's do this.'

She nodded, gratitude making her heart twist. 'I've got some documents for you to review.'

'Documents?' His eyes flickered over her face with a hint of mockery, but she refused to be intimidated.

'Given our individual wealth and asset base, legal protections make sense.'

'In case I ever try to take you to the cleaners?'

Her lips tightened. 'It wouldn't be the first time.' She unzipped her document wallet with force, removing the contracts.

She hated the sympathy she saw in Alex's face. All year, people had viewed her as a victim, but that was about to stop. She was going to show everyone not only that she'd moved on, but also that she was deliriously happy—and with Greece's number-one bachelor, to boot.

He reached for the contracts, skimming the first page, turning it, reviewing the second. 'This looks standard.'

She raised her brows. 'How many prenuptial agreements have you signed?'

'None.' He glanced at her. 'But enough contracts to recognise unaltered legalese when I see it.'

'I just downloaded a standard template and modified it slightly. The gist is just that we keep what we came into the marriage with. So if we were to divorce, neither would have a claim on the other's wealth.'

'Seems reasonable.' He paused as he turned the page. 'Is there anything in here about children?'

'No.' She hesitated, feeling as though she were stepping into the twilight zone. 'I've been thinking about that.'

His expression gave nothing away, but her tummy

suddenly squeezed as her nerves began to jangle. 'I know that's your condition for agreeing to this.' She spoke the words so quickly they all tripped over each other. 'And I agree to it in principle. But...' She paused, reaching into her briefcase and pulling out another document. 'There's something important we should discuss first.'

He waited with an expression that gave nothing away.

'I know your parents divorced, and that a lot of people do, and that's fine.' She missed the twisting of emotion deep in his eyes—her own feelings were taking too much space. 'But we're making a decision to get married specifically for the purpose of having children. I think it's only fair—to those children—that we agree to do everything we can to hold our marriage together. I would prefer not to share custody across our homes if we can find a way to live as husband and wife, come what may.'

'That seems fair.'

Her eyes widened. 'So you're saying you'd want to stay married?'

'Yes.' His eyes lanced her. 'My preference would also be to raise our children together.'

'What if you're miserable? Or I'm miserable?'

'Then we'll re-evaluate things. But as much as possible, we should go into this marriage with the intention of it being for good.'

Her heart leaped, and she tried not to be too pleased at the small victory. Everything with Jonathan had been a fight, all the time. She hadn't expected—or been prepared—for Alex to be so *reasonable*. Strangely, despite having spent a year fighting for divorce from Jonathan then a year recovering from it, she didn't feel at all nervous about what she and Alex had just agreed to.

As he continued to read, her cheeks flamed red, because she knew what the next section of her homemade contract dealt with.

'Sex on Friday night through Sunday night only.' It was obvious, when he lifted his face to look at her, that he was trying to flatten a smile. 'Never during the week?'

She shook her head firmly. 'I think it makes perfect sense to establish these—'

'Rules,' he supplied.

'Right.' She nodded, briskly.

'Uh-huh.' He turned the page, frowning when there was nothing further. 'There's no penalty clause.'

'I'm sorry?'

'Well, what happens if we slip up?'

'We won't,' she promised with complete confidence.

'I see.'

But Tessa had thought about this from every angle, and she knew this was the perfect way to contain the chemistry he'd referred to, to ensure it didn't boil over too much. 'This isn't a real marriage, and we're not really a couple. While I won't even attempt to deny that there's a spark between us, we're not animals, Alex. We can control when and where we act on it.'

'Of course,' he agreed, even when she had the feeling he wasn't agreeing with her at all, so much as teasing her.

She ignored the whip of frustration inside her belly. He could laugh and joke all he wanted; nothing would change Tessa's mind on this score. They had to take charge of this marriage, or it would never work.

'Do you agree to the contract?'

He ran a finger over the page and shook his head. 'It's a good start, but it could do with a bit of work.'

'Okay.' She reached for a berry, popping it in her mouth then wishing she'd resisted when his gaze followed the innocent gesture, lingering on the softness of her lips. Heat rushed through her.

'Where would we live?'

She looked around them. 'I'd actually been planning to suggest my apartment but...'

He waited, regarding her.

'I like your place. I can move in here, if that's easier.'

His eyes sparked with something she didn't understand. 'I will give you the full tour after this.'

Alarm bells dinged. A full tour would include things like bedrooms, and right now that was a dangerous prospect. 'That's okay, I can imagine,' she mumbled.

A knowing glint in his eyes showed he understood exactly what underscored her hesitation, but fortunately he didn't push it.

'We'll live here.' He made a note at the bottom of her contract. *Will.* Not *we could.* Something ignited in her bloodstream. This was happening. And even though she'd wanted this, it felt surreal and scary to contemplate the reality of becoming Mrs Alex Zacharidis. 'When will we get married?'

'Soon.'

'A week?'

'That really is soon,' she said with a shake of her head.

'I made enquiries this afternoon. I can get the legal documentation expedited.'

She bit down on her lip. What point was there in prevaricating? 'I guess that adds to the idea of this being a red-hot love affair.'

'As though we absolutely couldn't wait for the ink to dry on your divorce.'

'Yes,' she agreed, glad he understood.

'And we'll tell your parents together?'

'My parents.' She closed her eyes briefly, the main purpose for setting this in motion sharp in her mind. 'I'll call them soon. They should hear the news from me.'

'No.'

She blinked at him.

'I know your father, and he will only respect this if we do it properly. I'll ask for permission.'

She almost spat out her champagne. '*You'll* ask for permission?'

'What's the matter with that?'

'Apart from the fact I'm not an object of my father's to be given away?'

'He's traditional. It's about respect.'

'But you're *you*,' she reminded him.

'What is your point?'

'That you're the last man on earth to ask anyone for anything.'

'True, but the circumstances here are unique. My relationship with your brother, your parents... I can't ignore your father's wishes. I'll speak to him first.'

She hadn't expected this old-fashioned insistence and she had to remind herself it was just about respect of her father, nothing more.

'Good.' He turned the page of the contract. 'What kind of wedding do you want?' He peppered her with questions for the next hour, nutting out details she hadn't considered, until finally he dropped the pen and rocked back on his heels. 'That should do it.'

'Very comprehensive,' she agreed, wondering why the butterflies in her tummy seemed more excited than anxious.

'I'll have my office draft a press release tomorrow.'

'I've already done it,' she said, aware of the look on his face that spoke of being impressed. 'But what I don't have is a photo of us. It would be better if we could submit the press release with some kind of image. Do you mind if we take a selfie?'

He looked at her for several beats. 'Of course not. Mind if I see it?'

'The press release?'

He nodded once.

She reached into her handbag and withdrew a final piece of paper, handing it to him with fingers that shook slightly.

Theresa Anastakos announces engagement to Alexandros Zacharidis

'Well, for a start...' he paused '...I'll make the announcement.' He grabbed his pen and drew an arrow from his name to hers, indicating that they should swap.

'Why? Because you're the guy?' She almost poked out her tongue.

'Sure.' He shrugged his shoulders as though submitting to such outmoded patriarchal ideas wasn't innately offensive. 'And because you want your ex to seethe with jealousy. So, let's make it seem like I've pursued you, and finally won you over. How about…?' He scratched a confident line through the title. *"'Alexandros Zacharidis is delighted to announce engagement to Theresa Anastakos"?'*

Her heart did a little flutter, but she nodded curtly, as though it was an insignificant detail. 'Sounds good.'

He continued to read:

"'After a brief courtship, Theresa Anastakos is pleased to announce—'" He paused, put the lid on the pen and then shook his head.

'On second thoughts, this is way too stilted.'

'Well, what do you want me to do? How should we say it?'

He withdrew his phone from his pocket and clicked a few buttons, then let out a low whistle. 'You have a heap of followers on Instagram. Why not just announce it there?'

'Instagram?' She shuddered, the idea of social media covering her skin in goosebumps. The whole concept of social media was to put oneself out there, to exhibit and display, and beyond a few photos of artworks she'd been particularly proud of, Tessa had never taken to using the communication medium much at all. 'I'm not really into it.'

'I can see that. But regardless, you have many followers, and major news networks are bound to pick it up.'

'I guess that's more in keeping with what people do,' she agreed anxiously.

'So why don't we call your parents now and let them know, then you can post a photo and be done with it? My company will share any post you make. News will get around swiftly.'

Her heart stammered. 'So soon?'

'This was your idea, right?'

'Yeah, I just…'

She felt his eyes burning into her and had to confront the truth of their situation.

'Honestly? I really didn't think you'd say yes.'

'Nor did I,' came the swift response. 'Yet here we are, engaged.'

They stared at one another with a strange, shifting sense of fatalism, as if only now coming to grips with the fact this was really happening.

'So let's make it official.' He slid her phone across the bench, eyes on hers, holding a challenge. He was right. There was no sense putting this off a moment longer. Her parents would be thrilled, and that was all that mattered.

CHAPTER FOUR

THE MOMENT SHE hit 'post' on Instagram, events were set in motion.

She muted notifications on her phone, then turned it off when the calls started coming. First from friends, then from acquaintances, and finally from the media who, somehow, always managed to be able to get hold of private mobile-phone numbers.

After that, there was barely time to breathe. From the choosing of a wedding dress to confirming all the details in a hurry, to the delivery to her home of the most stunning engagement ring she'd ever seen, every minute of every day of that one single week jettisoned her towards this afternoon, a sunny Friday, on the bow of Alex's mega yacht, surrounded by a select handful of friends, and the only family they had remaining—her parents. Their presence as both Tessa and Alex's only blood relations underscored his personal motivation in making this marriage happen, highlighting how small their family connections were.

It was a week beset by uncertainty for Tessa. Was she doing the right thing? To launch from one marriage to another seemed like a particularly stupid idea. But then, just when her doubts almost had her convinced to abort the entire plan, she'd catch sight of her father's expression, his smile, his relaxed state, and she knew that this was worth it. If Jonathan had been her rebellion, then Alex was the path to repentance.

Some gossip rags continued to run whatever salacious detail Jonathan revealed on the reality TV show, which made it even easier for Tessa to convince herself she was doing the right thing. This marriage would put an end to Jonathan's hold over her, once and for all.

Every detail of the ceremony was perfect. Her father walked her down the aisle, beaming this time, in contrast to the stilted way in which he'd led her to the altar the last time she'd attempted this. The group with whom they'd chosen to mark the occasion were people with whom they could relax, and the ceremony itself was blessedly brief—because, as much as Tessa knew she was doing the right thing, that didn't stop her from feeling almost suffocated as the formalities went on.

The vows were recited in full, and then, out of nowhere, the reverend uttered those well-worn words, catching Tessa completely unaware.

'You may now kiss the bride.'

She startled, eyes wide and flying to Alex's face, as she grappled with this turn of events and kicked herself for not having pre-empted it. Of *course* they'd have to kiss—and look to be enjoying it.

Conscious of their guests watching, smiling, unaware that anything was amiss, she lifted a hand to Alex's chest, her fingers splayed across his pectoral muscles, as if to hold him at a set distance—or perhaps to draw him closer? There was no time to analyse her intent. A second later, his hands lifted to capture her face, one on either side, big and strong so her cheeks were completely covered and she was both trapped and caught, neither word holding negative connotations for Tessa.

He angled her face and his eyes lanced hers, mocking, questioning, and finally warning, as he dropped his head lower. His breath brushed her mouth first, warm and heady, so her lips parted of their own volition, and the hand in his shirt tightened, holding on to him for dear life. He dropped lower, his lips brushing hers, teasing her, tempting her, so she moaned, low in her throat, as a thousand memories, wishes, dreams flew into her mind.

There were so many layers to her feelings for Alexandros. As a teenager, she'd loved him—as much as any teenager could love a man. He'd been the object of all her fantasies. Every night she'd lain in bed thinking of him, willing herself to dream of him—because in her dreams, he'd never notice their ten-year age-gap or how gawky she was. After Stavros, and their night together, he'd taken on a new significance, so that she was almost lost to the power of her memories and needs, quite destroyed by the absence he formed in her life, particularly after she'd known the sweet completion of being in his arms.

His total desertion had destroyed her.

She'd been desperate for someone to make her feel whole again. She'd wanted someone to replace Alex, she'd needed to overwrite him, to push him from her mind, and then, Jonathan had appeared, handsome and flattering, fixing her bruised ego with his compliments. She'd thought it was love even when, with the benefit of hindsight, she could quite clearly see it was more a matter of Jonathan loving her family's fortune.

All her complex memories of Alex washed over her as his lips paused against hers, so she was rammed by the past, the distant past and the tangle of the unknown future, and, out of nowhere, tears threatened to sting her eyes, because she needed this marriage to fix her life, not complicate it.

Had she made a deal with the devil?

For the sake of her father, yes, she had. And now she had to live with it.

She went to pull away, but just as she did so his tongue flicked out, moving between her lips, taunting hers, duelling with it, and she moaned, because on some elemental level, despite what she'd just been thinking, she wanted this, so badly. She ached for him, regardless of how he'd rejected her in the past, regardless of how he'd hurt her.

And what kind of fool did that make Tessa?

She swayed forward, her body melding to his, and then he deepened the kiss with a swift, hungry strength, taking her and turning her away from the guests, his kiss now private and intimate, promising a thousand things that were between the two of them, and no one else.

And just when she felt ready to melt into the deck he lifted up, his dark gaze holding her dazed eyes, and his arm came around her waist for support. Their friends and family cheered, standing to celebrate the new couple, but inside, Tessa was numb.

There was no way she could control this. For the first time since agreeing to this marriage—and his terms—she realised that she was just as powerless to control her feelings for Alex as ever before. She knew how that would end...she had to protect herself.

Alex made a short speech, and then there was cake, and champagne, and finally they returned to the shoreline to allow guests to depart, enabling the 'happy couple' to enjoy their wedding night on a boat that more closely resembled a penthouse on water.

Tessa offered Alex a cool smile to prove to him, and herself, that she was calmly in control of their situation, even when their kiss had left her with a thousand doubts on that score.

'Mrs Zacharidis,' he murmured, watching her and seeing far too much.

Her lips tightened. 'I guess it's official.'

He moved closer, his hand reaching for hers, so she frowned, because they weren't really a couple and they didn't need to pretend. But when his fingers curved around hers, it felt...right. *Careful, Tessa.* She couldn't trust these feelings. Nothing about this was right—it was simply a means to an end.

'Any regrets?'

She considered that a moment, then shook her head. 'You?'

'I never have regrets,' he said with classic Alex arrogance. 'You look stunning.'

She dipped her head forward. 'Thank you.'

'I like this better than what you wore to your last wedding.'

'You weren't there.'

'No, but your parents had a huge photo by the door.'

'It's gone now.'

'I know.'

'No doubt you'll be up there before tomorrow morning.'

He laughed with genuine affection and a pang of something like jealousy hit her right in the heart. His affection for her was genuine, there was no doubting that. 'I'm flattered.'

'They really love you.'

Something flickered in his eyes, a look she didn't understand, and then he turned his face away, eyes chasing the cliffs that formed a wall to the shore. They were white in colour, crisp against the perfect turquoise of the sea.

'On days like this, they miss him so much,' Tessa continued, her smile slipping. 'Stavros should be here.'

'Yes.'

And then it was Tessa who was closing the distance, coming to stand right beside him, their hands held at her side.

'I wonder what he'd make of this,' she asked with a small shake of her head.

'He'd want to kill me,' Alex responded with not a hint of doubt.

'Why? For swooping in and being my saviour?'

He angled his face to hers, his eyes sparking with unmistakable intent now. 'For the direction of my thoughts all week.'

Her lips formed a perfect 'o' and she didn't dare ask—she didn't *need* to ask—for clarification on the direction of his thoughts, because her own thoughts had gone there plenty too. She'd done her level best to keep busy, but in the back of her mind the fact they were to be married, and that a whole weekend stretched before them now, was like a form of hypnosis. If she didn't use all her concentration, she felt herself falling under the spell of those thoughts, wanting, more than anything, to remember every detail of that night.

'Are you hungry?'

The question was the last thing she'd expected. She shook her head without breaking eye contact; she couldn't.

'Do you want to go for a swim?'

Swimming? As warm as the weather was, it was the last thing on Tessa's mind. 'Do *you* want to go swimming?'

His eyes bored into hers and she held her breath, waiting for him to deny it, but then, earning a whip of frustration from Tessa, he nodded slowly. 'Why not? We've got all night.'

And just when she thought the moment was over, he leaned down and kissed her with the same kind of hunger he'd shown during their wedding ceremony, as though this was the end of their time together and not the beginning, as though he could commit the taste of her to memory. It was all a lie. She knew how important it was to remember that. Alex was a very practised lover—he'd had more experience than she cared to contemplate. He was capable of turning his passion on and off at the drop of a hat, but Tessa wasn't. She was nothing like him.

'Did you bring bathers?' He asked the question right into her mouth, so the words washed over her and she shivered.

She shook her head without breaking contact with his lips. 'It's our wedding, not a beach holiday. I… wasn't expecting us to stay onboard after… I mean, after the ceremony.'

'Then we'll have to swim inside.' He lifted her easily, cradling her against his chest and kissing her as he carried her along the side deck of the yacht and through a timber door.

She didn't notice anything as he walked, navigating the corridor with ease, passing rooms that could have been bedrooms or not, until he reached a large space that had a spa bath at the front of it. 'Oh.' She tried to subdue her butterflies into order as he carried her towards it. She tried to keep hold of her sensible thoughts, and, most importantly, the knowledge that even when things looked and felt perfect, they could actually be the exact opposite.

On the edge of the spa bath, he placed her down, his eyes meeting hers with a mocking challenge as he began to unbutton her dress, reaching behind her so their bodies touched and his lips were just an inch from his.

Did he know how much she wanted to reach up and kiss him?

Did he understand what he was doing to her?

Of course he did. This was Alex Zacharidis. He knew *exactly* the impact his purposeful seduction was having on Tessa.

As he put her in the swirling spa water, she reminded herself that relaxing into this relationship would be the first step on a path to disaster, and yet she didn't make any effort to remove herself from the situation. She simply watched, heart racing, blood firing.

He shucked off his shoes and shirt and trousers before stepping into the spa in only his boxer shorts, and then he was kissing her again, this time pulling her towards him as he sat, so she straddled him, her hair falling down her back in dark chestnut waves, every part of her singing at the perfection of this physical moment.

Tessa no longer believed she had a sensual bone in her body, so it was incredible to *feel* these responses, to know her body to be wanting him, and to feel evidence of the way in which he wanted her. After Jonathan, she'd presumed this part of her had been destroyed; feeling it stirring to life made her want to throw caution to the wind and make love to Alex, just to prove to herself that she was, in fact, capable of pleasure and pleasing.

Hunger drove her, making her ache to take him just like this, but he went slowly, slowly, chasing his fingers over her body, followed by his mouth, teasing her flesh with little flicks of his tongue then nips of his teeth, so sensual, so flirtatious, but nowhere near *enough.* Frustration made her growl because she didn't want to be taunted. She wanted to be made love to, right now. Every single one of her fantasies was barrelling through her. The week of waiting had been all the foreplay she needed.

'I want you,' she declared against his throat, grinding her hips to prove her point, shocking herself with the power of her needs and also her directness.

'That is something we share,' he grunted, rolling his hips in an answering rhythm, then moving his mouth to her breast, taking a nipple between his teeth and wobbling it before withdrawing and flicking it instead with his tongue. She arched her back as arrows of pleasure shot through her and he laughed softly, then bit down again, sucking this time, so she whimpered, because it felt so damned good and yet it was still not enough.

His touch was so sure, so confidently demanding, and yet she was tumbling out of control—and even when racked by passion, she was innately terrified as well, because control offered protection and she *had* to protect herself.

Tessa pulled away from Alex, face pink, eyes sparkling when they met his. 'But this is just sex, like we agreed in our contract.'

'Well, it is Friday,' he agreed, without missing a beat.

'Right.' The reassurance relaxed her, as much, at least, as Tessa was capable of relaxing in any circumstance like this. Her relationship with Jonathan hadn't been easy, and on the handful of times they'd been intimate he'd been so critical of her that she'd lost all confidence. It was so easy to believe she was terrible in bed. The insults he'd thrown at her when he'd turned to other women, the way he'd looked at her... The insidious voice of self-doubt was peppering her mind, so she pulled away, needing to know that this wasn't just a means to an end. 'You know I'm still on the pill, right?'

He paused, and ice infiltrated her veins, until he lifted his shoulders. 'Then this will not be the time we make a baby.' He pushed up, kissing the skin on the side of her mouth. 'But we can discuss contraceptives another time.'

Butterflies burst through her. So this wasn't just a means to an end, he wasn't using her desire for him to make a baby, yet she couldn't get self-doubt out of her mind regardless. Old habits were too entrenched, and she had too much to overcome. Yes, there was Jonathan's treatment of her, but at the root of it all, and the real reason Jonathan had been able to undermine her so successfully, was because of the way Alex had rejected her four years earlier.

The scathing way he'd looked at her, the way he'd spoken to her...

She would never forget it.

What if it happened again now? What if they slept together and then he responded in the same way? Panic exploded, so her brow beaded with sweat.

He kissed her hungrily, yet her pleasure ebbed, leaving only anxiety.

Sensing Tessa's shift of mood, he pulled away, frowning a little as he scanned her face. 'Are you okay, *agape*?'

Great. Just what she needed—kindness. From Alex. She blinked, turning her attention to the stunning view and pretending the kind of fascination that would befit someone who'd never before seen the ocean. 'I'm fine. Let's keep going.'

He made a sound of surprise, then moved, unseating her and shifting her to the tiled ledge beside him. Dark colour slashed his cheekbones, indignation carved his features into granite. 'This is not supposed to be a chore, Theresa. Contract or not, we do not have to have sex.'

Her eyes flashed to his, and her stomach tied itself completely in knots. Maybe her first instinct was right, and he *didn't* want her after all. And just like that, the sting of tears threatened the backs of her eyes, so she blinked quickly, doing her best to push them away. 'It's okay,' she said, as though it didn't matter. 'I don't mind either way.'

When he didn't respond, she blinked towards him quickly, in time to see his jaw shifting as though he was grinding his teeth.

'You're annoyed with me?' Just like Jonathan. This was a disaster.

'No,' he answered quickly, frowning. 'I'm confused by you, but that's okay.'

He had every right to be confused. A minute ago she'd been kissing him as though her life depended on it, and now she was completely devoid of desire.

'It's been a really long time for me,' she whispered, unable to meet his eyes.

'That's all right.' His gentle, kind response physically hurt her. She felt vulnerable—which she hated—and his kindness was just evidence that he saw her vulnerabilities and was taking pity on her. She almost groaned in frustration.

'No, it's not. I agreed to this. I can do it.'

'*Cristos*, Theresa, I don't want you to grit your teeth through sex. What the hell do you take me for?'

His offence was obvious. She grimaced, offering an apologetic smile before pushing up to stand on feet that were none too steady. She was a mess. She hadn't thought this through before—she hadn't been capable of thought—but as she looked around, she saw no towels and a perfectly nice floor she didn't want to saturate.

'I don't want to leave puddles everywhere.'

'It's a yacht—puddles go with the territory.'

She didn't respond. The idea of walking, dripping wet, away from him was undignified and somehow wrong.

'I'll get you a towel.' As he stepped out of the spa, the evidence of his own arousal was on display, so she turned her back, lips parted, breath burning. She was beyond confused. If he was aroused, then it was proof that he had wanted her. But maybe that was just a physical response, like sneezing when you looked at the sun.

Plagued by self-doubt, she hated herself in that moment, and everything that had happened to turn her into this. Wasn't there a saying about time healing all wounds? Maybe eventually she'd be herself again.

Alex returned with the towels, but instead of handing one to her, as she'd expected, he placed one on the floor at his feet and gestured for her to step out. She did so, not able to meet his eyes, and when she was standing in front of him he wrapped the other towel around her shoulders, making her feel warm and protected and safe. All feelings she immediately pushed aside. She was none of those things because of him. She had to find her own way to those emotions, she couldn't rely on Alex to provide them.

'Thank you.' Her gratitude was expressed crisply.

A sharp sigh escaped his lips and then he was lifting her up again, cradling her wet body to his broad chest, carrying her through the yacht. They were definitely leaving the puddles she'd intended to avoid, but she clung on to Alex, breathing in his masculine scent as he turned and walked through a door, into a bathroom that was too grand to exist on a yacht. Her family's own boat was well-appointed but this was next level.

He placed her on the tiled floor, holding her right in front of him. 'May I?' he asked, hand lifting to the back of her bra.

She couldn't look away. Eyes huge in her face, she nodded slowly, then blinked her eyes closed as he unclasped it.

He dropped it to the ground and her nipples puckered against the evening air, her skin lifting in goosebumps: not because she was cold, but because she was warming up again, finding it hard to keep a grip of the reality she so desperately wanted to have uppermost in her mind.

It would be so easy to lean forward and kiss him. To throw caution to the wind and surrender to their passion as they'd done earlier, but doubts collided with her absolute need to control the terms of their relationship, so instead she took a step backwards, looking over her shoulder. 'Is there anything I need to know about operating the shower?'

A lump formed in her throat and she looked away, conscious of the way he moved to the enormous shower and stepped inside, flicking a lever then sliding another one. 'This does temperature,' he said. 'And this, water pressure.'

'Okay, thanks,' she mumbled nervously.

'Do you need anything else?'

It was a loaded question with one answer. She needed him. But she needed, even more than that, to push the past from her mind. She just didn't know how. Marrying Alex had made sense on the day, but she hadn't realised that she'd be living with—making love to—the man who'd broken her heart and destroyed her self-esteem. She honestly believed she'd got over it, but the more the idea of sleeping with Alex became a reality, the more her fears bubbled to the surface, convincing her he'd reject her all over again. And how sharp would the sting of pain be this time?

'No. I won't be long.'

CHAPTER FIVE

THE DUSK SKY was filled with shards of light, splintered from the slow-falling sun like arrows of gold against a mauve and peach background. Stars were just beginning to spark overhead, and the air tasted of salt and summer. For the first time in years, her fingers itched to capture the scenery on a canvas. She closed her eyes for a moment, imagining the colours she would blend to distil exactly the right shade—it went beyond the colours for Tessa, it was about translating the atmosphere of that moment into a picture.

But with her eyes closed, her mind moved from the image of the sunset to the man at her side, silent and strong, haunting her not with anything he'd done, so much as just by his nearness.

Her eyes jolted open, and she turned to face him, the suddenness of the gesture drawing his face to hers. She frowned slowly, nerves fluttering inside her.

'Alex,' she said, his name hovering in the air between them, a little uncertainly. There was so much she didn't know—questions she should have asked before marrying him suddenly erupted as a volcano.

His features prompted her to continue, then he reached for his beer, removing it from the nearby counter and taking a sip.

'If…' She paused, the words seizing in her throat. She forced herself to continue. 'If we were to have kids, how would you see that working?'

'Do you mean the biology of falling pregnant?'

Heat flooded her cheeks. 'I meant the parenting, not the pregnancy part.' Though the thought of growing round with his baby was doing strange things to her equilibrium, and now the idea of children wasn't a strange, abstract concept, but a reality that was hovering just ahead of them. She could even imagine what their children might look like, with his eyes and symmetrical features and her glossy brown hair.

'We'd make it work.'

She bit down on her lip. 'That's a little simplistic, isn't it?'

'What exactly are your concerns?'

'You work a lot, right?'

He dipped his head in agreement.

'So you'd barely see our child?'

'My intention would be to scale back, once the baby was born.'

She angled her face, focusing on the disappearing sun.

'That doesn't suit you?'

'It's not that.'

'Then what?'

'I just…remember how busy my dad always was. And then Stavros. I know you're just like them…'

'Yes,' he said quietly. 'But I'm not asking you to have and raise my baby. I want children so I can be a part of their lives.'

'You keep saying children, not child. Why?'

She turned back to him just in time to catch the hint of a frown on his face. 'Why not?'

It was an unsatisfying answer, but she let it go.

'Did you have a nanny?'

He opened his mouth to respond, then closed it again. 'No.'

That was strange. 'But?' she prompted, reaching across and taking a sip of his beer, because her champagne was empty. Only just realising, he reached for the bottle and replenished her glass, his face averted from hers.

'There is no "but".'

'I got the feeling you were going to say something else.'

'No.'

'So your parents were active in your upbringing?'

He lifted his beer to his lips, taking a long sip, and she shivered because a moment earlier her lips had been on the bottle, and in a strange way it almost felt like they were kissing by proxy. Flashbacks of the way he'd kissed her in the spa sent her pulse into overdrive.

'Until I went to boarding school.'

'That was after the divorce,' she murmured, almost embarrassed by the little biographical details she had stored in her brain. As a teenager she'd been so in awe of him that she'd sat on the edge of her seat, listening to every word he said.

'A week after they told me they were separating.'

'That must have been hard.'

He ran his finger down the side of the bottle, apparently fascinated by the condensation. 'Not really.'

'You don't want to have this conversation, do you?'

'There's nothing to be gained by having it,' he confirmed, his tone unfamiliar to her, because for a moment, he didn't sound like a human so much as an automaton, devoid of emotion. But that wasn't Alex. Not really.

None the less, she let it go. 'That's a long way down the track anyway, right?'

He was quiet a moment, then turned to face her, speculatively. 'It's not essential that we conceive a child immediately, no.'

She considered that. 'How come you're not already settled down with some woman who's just as desperate to have babies with you?'

His lips twisted in a hint of amusement. 'Because until you came into my office with your very pragmatic proposal, I had no intention of getting married.'

'Why not?'

'For many reasons.'

'Such as?'

'Has anyone ever told you, you'd have made a great inquisitor?'

She wiggled her brows. 'Nope, but thank you.'

'It wasn't a compliment,' he murmured, but with the hint of a smile, so something warm zinged in the centre of her chest.

'You date women. I've seen the proof.' She tried

not to think about the photos of Alex Zacharidis that cluttered the internet, beautiful women hanging on his arm, coming in and out of nightclubs, so handsome, so desired.

'Have you?'

'Photos, anyway.' She shrugged. 'And you're obviously a very attractive, successful man.' The description emerged stilted. 'I'm guessing lots of women would be interested in becoming Mrs Zacharidis.'

'Would have been,' he corrected her tense. '*You* are my wife.'

You are my wife. The words were so possessive, so insanely hot, that her spine felt made of lava.

'Who knows?' he said after a beat. 'I never considered marrying anyone else.'

Her stomach fluttered. She ignored it, focusing on what he was revealing with his very spare answers. 'Why not?'

He compressed his lips with a hint of exasperation. 'You don't give up, do you?'

'Is it some big secret?'

He hesitated a moment, then shook his head. 'It's not something I generally discuss, but no, it's not what I would call a secret, either.' He finished his beer, leaning over the bar then, staring out at the ocean. In profile, his face was determined and strong. 'My parents' marriage was a living hell. Their very particular brand of love-hate was my purgatory from birth. I learned to walk on eggshells growing up, and I hated it. I was still a very small boy when I formed an intention to live on my own, always. I didn't want to fight the way they fought. I didn't want to know the tension of moving from love and tranquillity to hatred and rage.' His eyes burned across the horizon. 'They fought, always. And by that, I mean they almost killed each other. Shouted, cursed, accused, ranted, generally destroyed one another, until they'd make up and for a few days everything would be rosy, but not really, because it was like being in the eye of the storm. I only ever knew one thing for certain: the storm would keep going. They were incapable of being together without arguing.'

'You grew up in a war zone,' she murmured intuitively, so his eyes locked to hers, his expression grim, and then he nodded.

She shook her head wistfully for the boy he'd been. 'A lot of marriages *are* happy, though. Look at my parents'.'

'Your parents are very lucky to have found each other, but what they have is rare. Divorce is far more common. Present company included.'

'Ouch.'

'That wasn't meant to be an insult, so much as an observation. I would have thought you, of all people, would understand my perspective.'

She considered that thoughtfully. 'We didn't really fight like that.' Her finger went to the champagne flute and she curled her hand around it, distracted by the popping bubbles.

'What was it like between the two of you?'

She hadn't spoken to another soul about her marriage, but for some reason it didn't hurt to imagine opening up to Alex the way she thought it might have.

'We married very quickly,' she admitted, rushing the words rather than giving him any hint of *why* she'd been so eager to accept Jonathan's proposal, how desperate she'd been to overcome the hurt and embarrassment Alex had inflicted when he'd callously rejected her, but unconsciously she pulled away from him, putting distance between them as she remembered the pain he'd caused her. 'I'd known him a little over a month, and so I wound up married to a man who was, in many ways, a stranger to me.' She gnawed on her lip, hating to remember that time.

'Why get married so fast?'

Trust Alex to pinpoint the one area she wasn't comfortable discussing.

'I thought I was in love,' she lied, shooting him a cynical look. 'Why wait?'

'It's prudent to get to know someone, I would have thought.'

'Hindsight is a wonderful thing,' she muttered, then sighed. 'The truth is, there was a part of me that wanted to escape.'

'Escape what?'

You, she wanted to shout, *and the grip you had on my every waking thought.*

'Oh, a lot of things,' she mumbled. 'After Stavros, my world felt tipped off balance.' She couldn't meet his eyes. 'I lost my brother, and essentially my parents, who were so fogged by their own grief that they refused to let me leave the house, lest something happen to me, at the same time as they barely acknowledged my existence because they were in such a daze.

They've always been very protective of me, and that got a thousand times worse afterwards. Jonathan offered a way out—from all of it.'

He was quiet, considering that, but if he wondered, in the back of his mind, if any part of her decision was a reflection on him, he didn't ask the question.

'And yet you stayed married to him?'

'I wasn't miserable at first. All marriages have challenges and I thought we had to overcome ours. But some problems were too big to solve. We officially separated after two years, though we had been living basically separate lives for some time already. And then a year after that, we divorced. It was a…difficult time.'

Alex was quiet for so long she presumed the conversation had moved on, and she listened to the gentle, rhythmic lapping of the water against the boat's pearlescent sides. 'Do you still love him?'

The question zapped her, coming as it did almost out of nowhere. 'No.' A harsh rebuttal. Too harsh? 'Definitely not,' she added for good measure.

But when she turned to face Alex, there was cynicism in his eyes, as though he didn't, for a second, believe her. And maybe that was a good thing? If he believed she still partly loved her ex-husband, he'd never have reason to suspect he'd hurt her so much four years earlier, that she was still hurting from his words.

'In my experience, only deep love can cause such lasting hurt.'

She flinched, because he was right, but it hadn't been Jonathan she'd loved and been hurt by.

Eager to change the subject before he could ask anything more insightful, she said, 'I suppose we should be getting back to the marina.'

'Actually, I want to take you to Epíneio.'

'Where's that?' She immediately liked the musical name.

'My island.'

'Your island?' She arched a brow. 'Seriously?'

He nodded once, eyes returning to the sea. 'Is your ex-husband the reason you didn't have children?'

'Oh,' she chased an airplane across the sky with her eyes, 'I guess so.'

'Because it was so tense between the two of you?'

'Yeah.' There was no real need to elaborate on that. She sighed softly. 'Let's not talk about Jonathan, Alex. I don't want him in my life any more, and I sure as hell don't want him in our marriage. He's not relevant.'

She could tell, from the look in his eyes, that he didn't believe her.

Epíneio meant haven, and as his yacht drew closer to a small pontoon Tessa couldn't help thinking how apt the name was. Even from the deck of the boat, she could see the calming quality of the place. Tall white cliffs tufted with dark green grass and spiky trees gradually lowered to form a white sand beach with a thick wall of overgrown trees, creating the impression of nature run amok, and through the busy, ancient trunks she caught fleeting glimpses of a home—too fleeting to see much detail, so curiosity and anticipation filled her belly.

It was more than the scenery though. There was something exquisitely transient about the light, and again her fingers craved the familiar grip of a paint-brush, her artist's mind analysing the textures and shapes, the colours, imagining exactly how she could capture this natural palette.

As the crew brought the boat into the dock, expertly guiding it to the pontoon's edge, Tessa stood with her elbows propped against the railing, warm breeze lifting her hair, eyes trained on the island. She hadn't seen Alex for hours. They'd shared coffee that morning, and made some necessary small talk to break up the silence. It was all so…polite. Sitting across from him, she could never have guessed how close they'd come the day before to making love. Except for the way her pulse trembled when his eyes hooked to hers, and heat seemed to be burning her from the inside out.

As the boat achieved its resting position, the crew sprang to life, throwing down ropes and leaping onto the deck, to unfurl a walkway that would make it easier for Tessa and Alex to depart.

Alex appeared almost magically at her side, and the sight of him like this caused her heart to clench. He was wearing a white shirt and knee-length shorts, with glasses tucked into the collar of his shirt and a cap on his head, so Alex was so casual and handsome that her bones turned to puddles and she almost forgot about the distance she needed to keep from him and threw herself into his arms.

Instead, she offered him a small, tight smile. 'This is very nice.'

Nice? So tepid! She had become used to keeping much of herself screened off, and it hadn't bothered her.

In fact, she'd been grateful to have developed that technique, but for a moment she wanted to crack through that veneer and just be…herself.

'It's a good place to come when I need to get away.'

'And how often is that?'

He put a hand in the small of her back, simply to guide her towards the walkway, but that didn't matter. He might as well have been cupping her breasts, for the way her central nervous system went into overdrive. 'Most weekends.'

The narrow width of the gangplank brought their bodies close. She suppressed a shiver. 'Really? I thought you were out with a different woman every night?'

'And that bothers you?'

Damn it! She'd walked right into that. 'Of course not,' she responded stiffly. 'I suppose you come here with them, anyway.'

'No.' His interruption was sharp. 'Epíneio is personal. Private.'

A shiver ran down her spine, because he'd brought her here regardless, to his private sanctuary. It didn't mean anything, but something fluttered inside Tessa's belly; she felt ridiculously pleased.

From this vantage point, she could see more of the house and it forced a small sigh from her lips, because the building had clearly sat in this very position for a long time. Terracotta walls that had been rendered white were offset by a red-tiled roof. The door was painted a happy blue, and big pots of geraniums stood on either side. Everywhere she looked was a scene she wanted to capture. Excitement bubbled through her blood. During her marriage, she'd struggled with her art. Jonathan's criticism and her deeply unhappy state had paralysed her, but here, she felt inspiration at every turn.

'This is beautiful,' she whispered, the words utterly inadequate for the perfection that surrounded them.

'What about you, *agape*?' he asked with a note of determination.

Her eyes skittered to his and her heart thundered. 'You don't have to call me that, you know. No one is around. When it's just the two of us, we can be ourselves.'

'Okay, Theresa. Is that better?'

No, it was way worse, because he said her name like a whisper, and it hit her as a warm breeze on a spring afternoon, so she tingled all the way to her soul.

She was mesmerised by him, unable to look away. 'No one calls me that.'

'Stavros used to.'

Her stomach tightened. 'I know.'

'Whenever he would talk about you, he'd call you Theresa.'

Her lips twisted in an involuntary smile. 'What sort of things would he say?'

They moved from the jetty to the warm white sand, and because it was dry and uneven she almost stumbled. Alex's hand shot out, capturing her elbow, holding her close. She didn't pull away at first—the support was appreciated—but once they moved beyond the sand, under the shade of the coastal trees, she took a step to the side, her equilibrium in tatters.

'He was very proud of you,' Alex belatedly answered her question. 'He believed you were going to set the world on fire. In a good way,' Alex added, a small grin changing his face completely so the world seemed to tip off balance, and not just because of the unexpected compliment.

'Stavros? I don't believe it.'

'Surely you know he thought the world of you?'

Her lips twisted to the side. 'We were chalk and cheese,' she said after a beat. 'He was always talking about the company with my parents. The way his brain worked… I was in awe. Honestly, I didn't even know if he noticed me, half the time.'

Alex made a strangled noise of surprise and stopped walking. 'Don't say that.'

She looked up at him, his reaction unexpected. 'I loved him very much,' she hastened to add. 'I worshipped him, in fact.' She'd worshipped *both* of them. 'But I'm ten years younger, and we had nothing in common.'

Alex's chest moved as he drew in a breath, and awareness heated Tessa's veins. 'He was very protective of you,' he said, after a beat. 'He thought you were smart and determined, but far, far too kind. That your kindness would make you vulnerable.' A muscle worked overtime in Alex's jaw. 'He wanted to protect you from the worst of the world.'

That wasn't new information, and his protectiveness had driven her crazy, much of the time, but she still loved how much he'd cared. 'I miss him,' she said on a soft sigh.

'As do I.'

He put a hand in her lower back, guiding her once more along the path towards the house, and as it came into view, thoughts of anything else shifted from the forefront of her mind.

'Oh, Alex. This is stunning!' she exclaimed, genuinely moved by the perfection of the unassuming little house in the middle of an expanse of green grass. 'It's just what a beach house should be!'

She was unaware of the way his eyes rested on her face, his gaze hungrily travelling her features, reading her in a way she wouldn't have wanted to be read. Tessa was far too absorbed in the building, the geraniums and lavender and frangipani trees that formed a relaxed garden at the front, and the citrus she could see growing down the side. 'I can see why you come here so often.' She quickened her pace and unconsciously pulled away from him, moving up the stairs of the house with eyes full of wonder.

'It's an easy commute,' he said with a shrug, leaning across her to point across the garden. 'There's space for a helicopter, and, on the other side of the island, cabins for staff.'

'How many staff?'

'It varies depending on the season. In summer, just a couple—my housekeeper and gardener. She stocks the fridge with meals, he keeps the vines from taking over.' He gestured to the jasmine that was creeping advantageously along one side, reminding her of the story of Sleeping Beauty.

She sighed, the warmth on her back and the fragrance of the garden relaxing her in a way she would usually have fought against.

'I can already tell, I won't want to leave,' she joked, moving up the steps. They were uneven from years of use, their middles gently dipping like a hammock.

'You don't have to leave.'

But she bristled against that intuitively. She couldn't let herself get caught up in the fantasy of this. Because it was so easy to see how she could stay here and relax, how the beauty of this place would convince her— easily—to let her guard down. How she could let him call her *agape* and hold her close, kiss her and make love to her, and she would start to believe that this was real. It would be so easy to *trust* him, when she knew that trusting anyone was a sure-fire way to end up getting hurt. 'It's beautiful, Alex, but it's not real life.' The words were stiff and heavy, reality tightening around her like a straitjacket.

'Then just enjoy the weekend, Theresa. Your *life* will be waiting for you, Monday morning.'

CHAPTER SIX

ALEX DIDN'T THINK of his parents that often, and he hadn't dreamed of them in years—not since his mother had died and his brain had thrown random, ancient memories into the mix, so each dawn had brought with it a sense of total disorientation as he tried to wade his way back to the right time zone and reality.

But on that night, alone in his bed on Epíneio, he dreamed of his mother, and his father, and their fights were as vivid in his mind as if they were happening anew. He dreamed of the worst night—the one when his mother had threatened to kill herself, and a twelve-year-old Alex had run from his room to find her, heart racing, chest hurting.

They'd been in the kitchen, his mother's face tear-stained, his father's resolute and unfeeling. His mother held a butcher's knife in her hands, the one she used to slice the tomatoes when they were ripe and just picked from the vines. 'I hate you so much,' she'd sobbed, lifting the knife higher.

Alex wasn't conscious that he had made a noise, but he must have, because his mother turned to face him, her eyes like a wild animal's, her body trembling with anger and shock, face contorted. Her breath was the only sound in the room, and then it grew harder and more forced as she dropped the knife onto the counter.

His father spoke first. 'Alexandros. Go back to bed.' The words were a command, barked from his body, but Alex ignored them, running to his mother and pushing her—pushing her away from the knife, trying to shake her out of the mood, trying to bring her back to him.

She was stiff, like a board, her eyes enormous, and Alex had the strangest sense that she didn't recognise him. He was losing her, or had he already lost her?

He woke, on the second night of his marriage, in the early hours of the morning, face wet with perspiration despite the open windows that rolled a soft, salty sea breeze towards him. He could taste the tang in the air and, on autopilot, he stood and walked towards it, hovering at the window for several beats, waiting for his breathing to calm, for the images to recede.

His marriage had brought certain issues to the forefront of his mind. The dreams were an unwelcome intrusion.

He knew from past experience that he wouldn't be able to sleep after the nightmare, and so he didn't bother trying. Instead, he strode from his bedroom, wearing just a pair of boxers, into the open-plan kitchen. The full moon was high in the sky, cutting a silvery beam through the trees and across the floor, so he only flicked on the little lamp above the range hood, pouring himself a glass of Scotch in a crystal glass then resting it, untouched, on the counter.

His mother hadn't killed herself that night, but she'd planted the seed of worry in Alex's mind, and from that moment he hadn't had a single encounter with her that wasn't framed by his concern—even the good memories were tainted by his understanding of her desperation, and his apprehension of what she might be capable of. When she did, finally, end her life, it was with no witnesses, no cries, and no one to push away the knife. Which wasn't to say Alex hadn't been left reeling.

His lips tightened as his thoughts turned to his wife, and the marriage from which she'd escaped. Theresa was a very different character to his mother, but that didn't mean that staying in a miserable marriage might not have led her to the same all-consuming depression that had dogged his mother.

The idea of Theresa suffering even a fraction of that amount left Alex with a strange taste in his mouth, like acid and petroleum. He threw back a generous measure of the Scotch, then kept his hand curled around the outside of the glass, his grip firm, his body wound tighter than a spring.

Once, he'd heard his father describe his marriage as 'the dark side of the moon', but it had taken Alex's growing into a man for him to understand the meaning. Their marriage was indeed dark, but it was beautiful too, silvery and perfect, all too briefly, and so they'd both fought for those moments, for the silver and light, enduring the waxing of the darkness for the brief periods of shimmering joy, ever hopeful the latter would come to dominate. It rarely did.

His parents had let their emotions dictate their relationship.

His father he couldn't help but blame. Where his mother had clearly, he saw now, been suffering from depression and anxiety, his father had refused to get her help, and he'd refused to let her go, when the marriage was so obviously one of the reasons she was in pain.

His mother hadn't had the strength to leave.

But Theresa had.

She'd realised that the way she was being treated was wrong, that she deserved better, and she'd packed her bags and left, despite the fact that was admitting to having made a mistake. Despite the fact her bastard of an ex-husband seemed intent on continuing to mar her happiness, just because he could.

Hatred flooded Alex at the idea of any kind of person who could behave that way. Love turned to hate, hopes dashed, enmity remaining. It was a common story—one he'd sworn he would never play a part in.

Which was why, as he finished off his Scotch, he couldn't help but feel glad that love wasn't—and never would be—a feature of this marriage. Somehow, they'd ended up in a near-perfect scenario, having negotiated terms that suited them both. True, their desire was inescapable, but even that they could tame.

Although it wasn't completely perfect, he thought, pouring another drink. This time he carried the glass out of the kitchen, onto the front porch, where he leaned against the railing, regarding the ocean. He could see only darkness, and a hint of seafoam on the tip of the rolling waves, as the milky whiteness of the moon formed an uneven line in the distance. Theresa hadn't got out of her relationship with Jonathan scot-free. Her reaction to their intimacy after their wedding had shown how much of a burden she still carried.

They'd slept together before, so he understood the desire that stirred in her veins, and all the ways in which she was a passionate, sensual woman, but now it was clear to Alex that she'd been hurt badly, her confidence shaken.

His mother had been broken by marriage, and so had Theresa—albeit in different ways. And as much as he wanted to *show* her how great sex between them would be, he needed her to get there first, on her own. He couldn't put his finger on why that was so important, but he knew it mattered, and he knew he would wait.

It was one thing to make a pledge to himself in the small hours of the morning to respect her boundaries and keep sex from becoming an issue, and quite another to be confronted by the sight of his newly minted wife in a shirt of his that exposed her tanned, smooth thighs and which clung to her body like a second skin courtesy of the fact she'd obviously worn it swimming. She lay draped over a sunlounger, face tilted towards the house, eyes closed, her dark hair pulled over one shoulder. She looked beautiful, untouchable and incredibly hot.

So much for good intentions. As all his blood pooled in a specific part of his anatomy, he walked towards her, glad his boardshorts were black and would go some of the way to hiding the evidence of his attraction. He moved until his shadow was cast over her face and then he watched, waiting. Slowly her eyes peeped open, locking to his, and a frown briefly tightened her features before she sat up, awkward and self-conscious, reaching for her towel and pinning it to her chest, as though instead of one of his business shirts, she wore nothing.

'Alex!' Her voice was croaky, her eyes huge, lashes clumped together by water. 'I didn't know you were here.'

'I wasn't. I just came outside.'

'Oh. It was such a warm morning and the pool looked so inviting, but I didn't have a swimming costume so I borrowed one of your shirts—I hope that's okay?'

Uncertainty made her voice husky, and he hated that. He didn't want her to be nervous around him.

'Of course. I'll have the housekeeper arrange some clothes for you today.'

'There's no need,' she denied quickly. 'If we go home tomorrow—'

'Monday,' he corrected, taking up position on the lounger beside her with the appearance of effortless calm. 'There's no rush. We could stay longer.'

'Oh?'

'Technically, it is our honeymoon.'

'Right.' She nodded, frowning though, uncertainty on her features. 'But that's not really necessary.'

'You said you love the island.'

'I do.'

Even as he pushed this point, he wondered what the hell he was doing. He hadn't planned to suggest they remain any longer than the weekend, but something about her inability to relax made him want to keep her here. Away from Athens, reality TV shows, ex-husbands and the real world.

'Let's play it by ear,' he said with a lift of his shoulders. 'We'll leave when it suits us to leave.'

She opened her mouth as if to argue then shut it again, pushing herself back on the sunbed and staring straight ahead, clearly ruminating.

'How's the water?' he asked after another moment had passed, the sun beating down on him, warming him to the core.

'Divine.'

'Did you try the ocean yet?'

She shook her head, turning to face him, her cheeks pink.

'Well? Shall we?'

She hesitated and he could tell her first instinct was to say 'no', so he stood, extending a hand, gently encouraging her, waiting while she waged an inner argument and then finally pushed her legs over the side of her sunlounger.

'Just quickly,' she huffed, as though annoyed with herself for agreeing. He hid a smile as they walked towards the beach, Tessa one step in front of Alex, keeping a wise distance. He suspected that the slightest touch would cause them both to burst into flame.

* * *

The water was utterly perfect. It should have been re-laxing and soothing, but Tessa was far too aware of Alex to let it be either of those things.

She was on edge, just as she had been all night, lying in a big bed with crisp white sheets and the sound of the waves causing an answering rush of blood through her body, making her want to do something really stu-pid and go in search of him.

In the small hours of the morning, she'd craved him. Human connection. Contact. But more than that, Alex. He'd awoken something inside of her; emotions she'd long thought dormant, or non-existent. Desire. Attrac-tion. Sexual curiosity. Feelings he'd kindled years ear-lier, that only he had ever managed to invoke.

Navigating them again now was a nightmare.

She'd clung to the contract she'd made him sign, to the rules she'd carved out, and tried to tell herself that it would all be okay. If they were to succumb to the temptation of sex, it would only be within the para-meters she'd specified. She could still control it. Ev-erything would be fine.

But as he hovered in the water beside her, so close she could reach out and touch him, brushing her fin-gertips over his naked torso and feeling the muscular ridges of his abdomen, she knew she was in way over her head.

Slowly she turned to face him, unable to resist at least that temptation. Her breath caught in her throat.

He was so...*elemental*. So tanned his skin was like mahogany, with water droplets forming rivulets over his strong arms, his dark hair brushed back from his brow, wet and catching the glint of the sun in its ends. He was completely at one with the ocean, the sky, the sun, and when he turned to look at her and their eyes met, his smile made her heart tilt off balance. She wanted to look away, but he was too magnetic, and so she let herself stare, a moment longer, just a moment, before she returned his smile, albeit curtly, and jerked her face towards the house.

'How long have you had this place for?'

If he was surprised by her abrupt change of conversation, he didn't show it. 'I bought it about ten years ago. I wanted a place to get away.'

'Why?'

He moved to stand in front of her, blocking her view of the house, forcing their eyes to meet, and her stomach squeezed, her nostrils flared as she inhaled his fragrance and trembled in response.

'I worked hard, played hard back then, too.' She remembered. She'd only been a teenager, but she'd been fascinated by her brother's best friend, by his charisma and charm, his incredible good looks. She'd loved it when stories ran about him online, or in the papers, and she could read what he'd been doing. He'd taken on an almost god-like presence to her. 'The island was removed from all that. Calm, and quiet. There were no bars here, no parties.'

'You didn't ever invite friends here?'

'No. Not my father. Not even Stav.' He moved closer, so there was only a small volume of salty water separating them. 'You're the first person I've ever brought to Epíneio.'

Her tummy flooded with butterflies and she pulled back through the water, just a step, just enough. He echoed her movement, so the distance between them didn't grow any greater.

'Why?' she asked unevenly, then, with more urgency, 'Why did you bring me here?'

A small frown creased his brow as he contemplated that. 'You are in need of a haven more than anyone I can think of right now.'

She tingled all over. 'I'm glad you did.'

'Are you?' His eyes drove into hers, pushing her to look inside her heart and be honest. 'I did wonder if you'd prefer to be back in Athens right now, blissfully ignoring me.'

'I don't want to ignore you,' she admitted with a gnawing sense of doubt in her chest.

'No?'

She shook her head, slowly, not sure what they were talking about, nor what she was conceded, but following her instincts.

He moved closer, so now they were touching, and she froze, because on the one hand, this contact was all her dreams coming true, and on the other, it was terrifying, so her body jolted, frightened by the immediate response she felt in her cells, and the strength of her need for him.

'I wish…' he said, then cut himself off, eyes holding hers, his expression inscrutable.

'What do you wish?' she prompted urgently, the

warm ocean lapping against her sides, their bodies brushing in the water, her pulse thundering.

He lifted a hand, holding it tentatively beside her arm before resting it on her shoulder, his gaze dropping to the sight of his dark skin against her fairer. 'That you'd never married him,' he said with dark honesty.

Her heart twisted sharply, but she refused to read anything into his admission. After all, they'd both said their one night together had been a mistake. It wasn't as though he was admitting some long-held unrequited love.

'He was bad for you,' Alex continued, moving his hand to the collar of his business shirt she wore, holding the fabric between his fingers. It billowed in the water, so she was secretly aware of her exposed belly, of how close to naked she was beneath the shirt, with just a flimsy pair of undies protecting her modesty. That knowledge was setting her soul on fire, dragging her closer and closer towards the desires she knew she ought to fight.

'Yes,' she said simply, because he had been.

'You deserve better than that.'

She wondered, in the back of her mind, if she should pull away from him. It would be the smart thing to do. She'd promised herself she wouldn't let things get out of control between them. She couldn't. If she surrendered to these feelings, she'd lose herself completely.

'Anyone does,' she said with a tight movement of her shoulders.

'You particularly.'

'Why?'

A frown flickered across his face and, rather than answering, he shifted closer, so his body pressed to hers, and every single inch of her was aware of the hard planes of his body, the warmth of his flesh beneath the waters of the Aegean, his skin supple and firm, hair-roughened on his chest, and covered in water droplets so she had an insatiable urge to lean forward and taste him.

'I was so angry after you left.'

'When?'

'The night we slept together.'

Her eyes widened, the change of subject unexpected, so she startled as though being awakened from a dream. 'Were you?' She dropped her gaze to the pristine water that lapped between them.

'I'd been so weak.' Her eyes lifted once more to his face, but the intensity of his stare sent little arrows of awareness through her, making it impossible to concentrate. 'Not only had I slept with you, but I'd also been your first lover. I felt as though I'd betrayed Stavros in the worst possible way.'

'You were his best friend. He probably would have been thrilled to think of us together.'

'No.' Alex shook his head emphatically. 'He was very protective of you and I was—'

'So much more experienced,' she finished unevenly.

'That's a polite way of putting it.'

She searched for a way to explain. 'That night, I was just so—sad…' Her lips twisted into a bitter frown. 'I wasn't thinking straight—'

'But I was,' he interrupted urgently. 'Or I should have been. I should have known better.'

'You were very clear that night,' she said, ice now running through her veins. 'You regretted it. You wished it hadn't happened.'

'Yes. For many years, I have felt that,' he admitted, dipping his head in silent agreement. 'But now, knowing that you went from my bed to his, I wish…'

Everything in her body ground to a halt as she stared at him, willing him to finish the sentence. 'Yes?' she said, when only the sound of water splashing filled her ears.

'I shouldn't have let that happen,' he muttered. 'I should have taken care of you…'

Her heart stretched almost to breaking point. On the one hand, she wanted to point out she was a woman of the twenty-first century, capable and in control. On the other, she wanted to push forward into his arms and rest her head on his shoulder and allow herself, just for a moment, to be cared for, as he'd said.

'Stavros would have wanted me to take better care of you.'

Her insides felt as though they were being compressed. She couldn't make sense of how she was feeling—a thousand different things at once now. 'I don't need rescuing,' she muttered on autopilot, because that felt familiar and important to tell him. 'I made my own choices, my own bed, and I lay in it for as long as I could manage. Jonathan was my mistake, and my problem to fix.'

'And our marriage is your solution,' he said quietly, scanning her face, a hint of disbelief in his question that frustrated her completely.

'It's certainly changed the story,' she said with a shrug, wondering at the flicker of something in the depths of his eyes. The news outlets had all printed photos of their wedding, the carefully selected images they'd released to announce their union.

'I'm glad.' Their eyes were locked, a strange tension buzzing between them, myriad thoughts and feelings unspoken, so despite the stillness of the afternoon, the water felt choppy.

'I would never have got involved with you back then,' she muttered, wishing that were true, pulling away from him, moving deeper into the ocean until she had to tread water to stay afloat. He stayed where he was a moment, a perfect bronzed god, his eyes watchful, his body still, and then he moved to follow her, his arms bringing him through the water with ease, until he was just a few feet away from her. He could stand easily, though.

'No?'

'You were too much what my parents wanted.' And despite the strange air of discord between them, a small smile twisted her lips.

'You have never seemed like the rebellious type, Theresa.'

'No,' she agreed, frowning. 'I'm not. Never. Except in that one way. Jonathan was my single act of defiance.' She tilted her chin. 'After Stavros died, I tried so hard to be everything I thought my parents needed me to be. I was terrified of putting a foot wrong, of failing to live up to who he'd been.' She bit down on her lip. 'But the way they tried to push me into a marriage with you...' She shook her head. 'It was too much. You were his best friend; you were, in my mind, his, not mine.'

'Even after we slept together?'

'Especially then,' she agreed, shivering as she remembered the way she'd been pushed away, the rejection Alex had put her through. 'If anything, that made me more determined to find my own way. I met Jonathan a week after we slept together, and a month after that he proposed.'

He nodded slowly, his eyes gently probing hers. 'I remember.'

Her heart gave a funny little stammer. 'You do?'

He lifted his shoulders. 'Call it male ego,' he said with a strange, throaty laugh. 'I didn't love how quickly you moved on, even when I felt guilty as hell for what we'd done.'

'You didn't exactly make me think you'd be interested in a repeat performance.'

'It wasn't possible.'

She flicked her gaze away, hating how easily he could hurt her, hating how much that night had pulled at her. She'd loved him. A childish crush had probably always been so much more, and that night they'd been drawn together by forces greater than either one of them. At least, that was how it had felt to Tessa.

'I meant nothing to you,' she said quietly. 'You can hardly have been surprised when I started dating someone else.'

'And did I mean something to you?' he pushed, picking up on her carefully worded explanation.

Her lips parted in surprise. Damn it! She'd been

careless. 'What do you think? Of course, I had a stupid crush on you.'

His jaw tightened.

'But I was just a girl.'

'Twenty-two,' he pointed out.

'And inexperienced and sheltered, thanks to my parents and brother. You were unlike anyone I'd ever known. But it wasn't real, Alex. None of that was real, and none of this is real.'

'The sex was real,' he responded sharply, surprising them both.

Her lips parted as she tried to think of how to respond. But Alex was there first, his voice low and determined. 'You are my wife, and you want me just as much now as you did then. You cannot keep running from this, Theresa.'

Her eyes swept shut, the delicious sound of her name on his lips driving shards of need through her. He was right, she was running, because the alternative scared her senseless. 'We've negotiated the terms of our marriage,' she said, forcing cold resignation into her tone. 'I have no intention of reneging on our agreement.'

'That's not good enough.' She wondered at the dark undercurrent to his voice. 'I'm not going to let you sleep with me and pretend it's all because of a contract.'

She pulled her lower lip between her teeth, wobbling it uncertainly, eyes huge in her face.

'In fact, I'm willing to cancel that condition of our marriage. Forget I ever suggested it.'

The colour drained from her face. Familiar feelings of rejection slashed through her. 'You don't want—'

'What I want,' he interrupted swiftly, closing all the distance between them and lifting her in one motion, so her body was pressed to his and her legs moved, of their own volition, to wrap around his waist, 'is for you to admit you want me as a woman wants a man. Not because of the grief we shared that night, and not because of some deal we made before we were married. I want you to listen to your body and accept the desire flowing through you.'

But how could she? Tessa had been so badly burned by Alex that night, and then Jonathan had only compounded her hurt. How could she surrender to this?

Deep down, she knew that he was right, but that didn't mean there was no danger here.

She wanted him, with all her soul, and not because of Stavros, not because of their marriage contract, but because her body yearned for him on an almost mythical level, only to confess that to Alex would make her far too vulnerable to the kind of pain she was determined to avoid.

'It's never going to happen,' she denied, her voice wobbly now, her words husky.

He stared at her, long and hard, and she tilted her face, lips parted, aching for him to kiss her, even when a part of her felt as though she was breaking apart.

'Never is a very long time, *agape*,' he said with a lift of his shoulders, dropping his hand so hers fell away likewise. Her body felt flushed by ice water. 'If you change your mind, you know where to find me.'

CHAPTER SEVEN

SHE WOKE UP even earlier the next morning, the sound of the rolling waves breaking through her light sleep, so she blinked into the soft light and pushed back the covers, deciding against trying to settle again. A strange, unfamiliar energy was bursting through her, and Tessa wanted to burn it off. She dressed quickly, pulling on a pair of shorts and a T-shirt—taken from the shopping bags the housekeeper had left in her room the afternoon before—and decided to go exploring. This was a beautiful island, and a walk out in nature was exactly what she needed to shift her focus away from her husband and the way they sparked off one another.

Tiptoeing through the house as though she were a burglar, she crept into the kitchen and pressed the button on the coffee machine, sliding a cup beneath the nozzle and waiting for it to pool out. She watched as it formed a thick black liquid in the bottom, then, when it had stopped, lifted the cup to her lips and swallowed gratefully, eyes closed, experiencing the hit of caffeine with all her might.

'Good morning.' His voice, deep and hoarse, set her pulse raging immediately and she spun quickly.

'Oh, hi.' Heat flamed through her at the sight of Alex in a pair of jeans and a white shirt that accentuated his tan wonderfully. *Never is a long time.* It sure felt like it already. 'Did I wake you?'

'No, I've been up a while.'

'It's only just gone six,' she pointed out.

'I wake early.' His expression was carefully blanked of any emotion.

'I see. Well, don't let me bother you. I was just about to go for a walk. I thought I'd explore the place a bit.'

'You want to see the island?' He regarded her thoughtfully.

Why, when he looked at her, did she feel as though her whole self was fully visible to him?

'Yes.' It was easy to be emphatic in response to that question. In fact, it was easy to be emphatic about anything, other than the desire that was flooding her veins.

'Then let me show you a better way to see it.'

It was on the tip of her tongue to demur, but dammit, there was an inherent weakness inside of her, a weakness she'd always felt around Alex, that made her contemplate that for a beat. 'I was just going to walk around a bit,' she said, unconvincingly.

His expression tightened, his eyes warring with hers. 'If you want to be alone, that's fine. For my part, I'd enjoy showing you the best parts of Epíneio.'

Her heart skipped a beat. He was saying what he wanted. He was telling her he'd enjoy spending time with her. Why couldn't she admit as much?

Because he'd burned her once before. She'd offered him more than her body and virginity that night: she'd offered him her heart. Not in words, but surely in every look, every touch. He hadn't wanted her—not her heart, nor her body, beyond what that one night had been.

And yet she was married to Alex now, and they had to find a way to be together, to be civil and mature. That would take time and it would take practice. Perhaps the more she was around him, the better she'd get at this.

'You can think of me as your tour guide,' he said casually, and despite the fact she felt permanently on edge around Alex, with her nerves completely helter-skelter, she found herself nodding. After all, it would be churlish to decline.

'If you have time.'

'I wouldn't have offered if I didn't.'

Whereas Tessa had been planning to set off from the house on foot and explore at a snail's pace, Alex had other ideas. Around the back of the house there was a garage, with an off-road car, a jet ski on a trailer, and a jet-black motorbike with shiny chrome features. Her heartbeat accelerated rapidly as he moved towards it, running his hand over the leather seat then turning to face her. Her eyes lingered on his fingers and their touch of the bike; it was impossible not to imagine those same fingers caressing her with that lightness and intimacy.

Her pulse was thready and she jerked her eyes away. 'Have you ever been on a bike before?'

Her smile was wistful. 'No.'

'Not interested?'

'It's not that.'

'Ah, let me guess.' He watched her closely. 'Your family.'

She sighed. 'They're so dangerous.'

'They can be, when ridden inexpertly.'

She almost laughed. It was so like Alex, so brimming with arrogance, to dismiss the dangers inherent to motorbikes, because he had so much faith in his own abilities. Then again, it was hard to doubt him when he spoke with such confidence.

'What do you think, Theresa? Are you afraid to ride with me?'

'Are you trying to goad me?'

He laughed softly, his eyes crinkling at the corners. 'Perhaps a little.' He strode to the wall and removed two immaculate helmets, shiny and dark. 'If you don't want to ride, we can go in the car.' He nodded towards the four-wheel drive. 'You can't reach as many places on the island, but it will still give you a good overview.'

Her lips tugged to the side as she considered the options. The problem wasn't that she didn't want to ride on the motorbike, it was how much she did. Suddenly the thought of straddling the powerful machine, her arms wrapped around Alex's waist, pushed her senses into overdrive. Resisting him would be a Sisyphean task. So why, why, why did she start walking towards the bike, eyeing it as though it were some kind of irresistible dessert?

'Promise you won't tell my parents?' she joked, earning a smile from him that made her feel as though the sun were shining all its warmth directly through her.

'Cross my heart.' He walked towards her then, helmet in hand, pausing a foot or so away, before lifting the helmet towards her head.

'I can do it,' she said, though in truth Tessa had no idea how to fasten a motorbike helmet.

He ignored her interjection, sliding the safety device onto her head and checking the fit. Even when he was satisfied, he didn't step away.

'I like doing your firsts with you.' There was no humour in his voice now, only a deep, gruff intensity that flooded her body with awareness and heat of an entirely different nature to the sunshine warmth his smile had invoked.

It was an inescapable reference to the night they'd slept together, and she felt as though she'd been plunged into a river of lava. Memories assaulted her from every direction, but his words were a contradiction to the pain of those memories. He hadn't liked anything about that night; he'd made that perfectly clear.

'So what do I do?' she asked, glad he couldn't see her pink cheeks through the dark tint of the helmet.

He returned to the bench to pick up his own helmet and secure it, then moved to the bike, straddling it easily with his long legs. 'Sit behind me,' he said simply, then revved the engine to life, so the thrum of power reverberated in the pit of her stomach and she felt a rush of daring and excitement.

She was glad he wasn't looking, because the motion of getting onto the seat was nowhere near as easy for her, particularly when she tried to keep her distance from him.

'Grab on,' he said, once she slid into place behind him, a leg on either side of his, so she was intimately aware of him regardless of how she tried to keep some small distance between them. 'Or you'll fall off,' he added over the low throb of the engine, giving her little choice but to wriggle all the way forward and wrap her hands around his waist.

On second thoughts, perhaps they should have taken the car. At least in the four-wheel drive, she'd have had her own seat, and a whole console between herself and Alex. She was opening her mouth to say exactly that when he gave the engine another rev and drove forward, straight out of the garage and onto the driveway. From that moment, Tessa's heart was in her mouth as adrenaline overtook her system.

There was a track she hadn't noticed before, because it was narrow, carved between grass, but it took them away from the house, higher up, along the edge of the island, until white cliffs formed a sheer drop beneath them, and unconsciously she held on tighter, as the terrain grew more beautiful and more threatening, as fear warred with wonder, and she had to take deep breaths to calm her wildly firing nerves.

The bike hummed beneath her, and Alex's warm, strong body was wedged at her front, so when she inhaled she caught a frustratingly light hint of his masculine fragrance and desire shifted through her at the provocation. Her hands pressed to his chest, feeling his strength and power, his muscular chest and steady heart, and as he steered, his arms brushed hers, so her mouth went dry and breathing became almost impossible.

He navigated the bike along the clifftops, far enough from the edge that she never felt in any real danger—she trusted him—but close enough to show the stunning view and death-defying drop. After circumnavigating the perimeter of the island for some time—though time no longer had any meaning to Tessa and she couldn't have guessed if they'd been five minutes or fifty—he reached a fork in the track and turned inward, taking them away from the edge of the island and towards a more wooded area. Olive trees grew wild, interspersed with citrus and bushes of geranium and lavender huddled chaotically wherever they could find land, so the grass was thin and dappled by only a hint of sunshine through the thick coverage of leaves. The temperature change was immediate, but Tessa barely felt it; her heat had very little to do with the beating sun. A movement to their right caught her attention and through the tree trunks she saw several goats, pausing in their grass chomping—another explanation for why it was so sparsely covered—to lazily regard the passing motorbike. Alex was driving with care, navigating a track that was mostly smooth but which, from time to time, presented a rock or branch, so Tessa had time to stare right back at the goats, smiling inside her helmet at their intelligent eyes and curious manner. Her hands moved of their own accord, feeling the ridges of his chest through his clothes, and she trembled because she wanted, all of a sudden, so much more.

The trees gave way once again to open grass and then another path along the other side of the island, but this time the cliffs dropped away, bringing them down to a small, perfect cove. Though it was difficult to track their progress, she'd guess they were directly opposite his home now, on the other side of the island. The patch of beach was like something out of a tourist brochure, with crisp white sand and rolling hills to shield it from view, creating the impression of being walled off from the world. The water was the sheerest shade of blue she'd ever seen, even for this part of the Aegean. He brought the bike to a stop, but didn't cut the engine immediately, so it continued to rattle between her legs, beneath her, shooting barbs of awareness into Tessa's body and making her want to act on the feelings that had been tormenting her ever since she'd arrived at his office and realised that whatever had driven her into Alex's arms back then was still between them, just as urgent and undeniable. But Tessa wasn't that woman any more. So much had changed in her life.

Despite the beating of a drum, convincing her that there was some form of inevitability here, just as Alex had said, Tessa fought that, dropping her hands away from him and flexing her palms. He turned off the bike then, and the silence, after the roaring of the engine, was almost overwhelming. Here, there was nothing but the occasional bird call and the gentle lapping of the water against the sandy shore.

'Ready?' he asked from in front of her, so she scrambled off the bike, trying to put physical distance between them as a defence against her treacherous thoughts.

'Yes, please.' Her response was prim, her face still hidden behind the helmet.

He removed his own first, and before he could reach out to do the same to hers she acted, curving her fingers around the equipment and sliding it off, relieved when it came easily.

He watched, his eyes skimming hers, and then he turned away, placing his helmet on the grass near the bike as he went. She did likewise. A few feet away he stopped walking to wait for her and she slowed a little, uneasiness coiling inside her belly.

She'd proposed this marriage because she'd wanted to fix the mistake she'd made in marrying Jonathan. Her parents had thought Alex would be the right husband for her, but they'd had no idea what had happened between the two of them. They had no idea that she'd offered herself to Alex and he'd rejected her—after taking her virginity. So instead she'd married a man they'd hated, who had subsequently dragged their family name through the press at every opportunity. Yes, she'd married Alex as a way of apologising to her parents, of saying 'you were right'. But deep down she had to admit, just to herself, that she'd also married him because she wanted to be close to him again. She'd fought that knowledge, but standing here, staring at him as the sun bathed them both in its golden light, she could no longer hide from the truth.

She'd walked into this willingly. She'd wanted him the day she'd gone to his office and she wanted him now.

It terrified her, but it also excited her, just like the

motorbike ride up here. Maybe the best things in life were always complicated and multi-layered?

'Come,' he commanded, holding out a hand. She eyed it warily for a second before, with a degree of fatalism, placed her own in his, shivering the moment their flesh met. It was just a simple holding of hands, but for Tessa, coming on the back of her realisation, it was so much more. It was as though they were saying their wedding vows all over again, even more so when their eyes met and locked and she felt, right in the centre of her heart, as though something was stitching back in place inside of her.

It was the magic of this place, that was all. The island stood on its own, unfazed by humanity and heartbreak, by hurt and dishonesty.

'It's beautiful,' she said, because it was true but also because she needed to break the intimacy of their connection.

'It's private.'

And again she had the sense that his own privacy was something he valued immensely. She tilted her face to his, staring at him until he turned to look at her, his eyes lighting little fires beneath her skin.

At the edge of the beach he kicked off his shoes, waiting for her to do likewise, then taking them onto the white sand. She yelped as the heat caught her off guard. She began to hop and then Alex lifted her easily, throwing her over one shoulder as a caveman might his quarry, carrying her towards the lapping shore and placing her on the cooler, wet sand, sliding her down his body so every single inch of her was aware of every single part of him and her brain was filled with floating shards of glass, blades of awareness punctuating the perfection of this day.

There were a thousand reasons why she wanted to keep her level head, to hold on to her reasons for resisting this—and him—but there was also the beating of a drum, drawing her towards him, so the past, her marriage, their one night together, all seemed to fade into nothing—concerns carried away by the gentle drawing of the ocean, now in the custody of the deep sea beyond.

He didn't move. His body—strong, powerful, safe—stood like a sentry, but Tessa couldn't fight this any longer. She was shaking from the effort of resisting him, her whole body in meltdown. She wanted him, so badly, and that terrified her, so she could only lift a hand to his chest and press it there.

Her eyes sought his, probing him, asking him to be gentle with her, begging him not to hurt her again, because Tessa wasn't sure she could bear that again.

And yet, wasn't this paved with pain? Alex was not like Jonathan. She'd never felt anything like this for Jonathan—that was why she'd chosen to marry him. Because he was completely non-threatening. She'd never felt her senses shuttling into overdrive with Jonathan. She had never lost sleep over desire, never dreamed of him. Everything about it had been reassuringly lukewarm, until he'd started to belittle and demean her, until he'd begun to cheat on her. She knew now that her pain had more to do with the realisation she'd made a terrible mistake, rather than any hurt feelings over Jonathan's lack of love for her.

But with Alex, the threat was so much more real.

If she let herself go with him, if she *really* let herself go, and forgot the contractual nature of their deal, she was terrified she might lose her heart as well as all of herself. Alex was a man determined not to love. She might give her heart to him, but he'd never return his own; the effects of that would be devastating.

The smartest thing of all would be to pull back from him. To push space between them, to take several deep breaths and remember that the worst thing she could do was become swept up into their relationship, to forget, even for one single moment, that this wasn't real.

'Alex…' She tried to find the words to explain, to tamp down on the sense of building urgency, but he was so close and the war raging within her felt a lot like a losing battle.

'Yes?' He was so close. Their bodies were almost as one, and the heat of the day was nothing to what they were generating. Did he feel it too? She had to believe he did. After all, he was the one who'd argued for their relationship to become physical.

And if he was disappointed by her? If Jonathan's insults held water? *'You are just incredibly lacking in sex drive. Can you blame me for looking elsewhere?'* She flinched, as though the words were being rained down on her in real time, and her central nervous sys-

tem began to quiver, because she was enraged and
filled to the brim with desire, needs flooding her, so
she dug her fingernails into his chest, as though she
could stem this from getting out of control, if only she
held on hard enough.

'What is it, *agape*?'

She didn't argue with his use of that term. She bit
down on her lip, eyes holding his, so there was nothing
for it but to be completely, openly honest.

'I'm scared, Alex. I feel—' She searched for words
that could describe all of her angst and fears and shook
her head when they didn't come. 'I don't want to get
hurt again.'

A muscle jerked in his jaw as he dropped his head,
his lips brushing her hair. 'I'm not going to hurt you.'

'You don't know that.'

For a long stretch of time only the sound of wind
rustling through the nearby trees broke the silence, and
then, his voice, deep, gruff and steady: 'Would you like
to go back to the house?'

She stared at him, frustration swishing through her
at the very idea, and she shook her head. She was sick
of being careful. Sick of listening to the fears that had
become embedded in her. And most of all she was
sick of ignoring the basic, physical needs of her body.

'No,' she ground her teeth together, aware that she
was about to admit to something quite mad, and unable to care, 'I don't.'

His eyes flickered with curiosity and speculation
and then Tessa was moving, no longer able to resist

temptation, no longer caring for the consequences. It was impossible to think this wouldn't complicate things; it was also impossible to care.

CHAPTER EIGHT

SHE MOVED QUICKLY, as though jumping into a pool, throwing herself at him with all her body, lifting her lips to his at the same moment he wrapped his arms around her waist and pulled her against him, kissing her right back, his mouth dominating hers, claiming it and holding it. Shards of something like certainty burst through him, because something about that kiss on this beach felt a thousand kinds of right and he knew then that he'd brought her here for this exact reason. Not because he'd thought they'd have sex, but because there was something so pure and right here, that it felt like a place to be free of all the restrictions that had been dogging them ever since she arrived in his office and suggested this marriage.

His tongue duelled with hers, tasting her, flicking her mouth, as his hands drew her down onto the sand, a fierce need erupting inside of him, demanding more, making him want her a thousand times over, so he rolled her onto her back, the water lapping gently at their feet as he kissed her, tasting her sweetness and being deluged by memories of that long-ago night when a similarly urgent need had rolled through them.

She made a whimpering noise that sent his senses into overdrive, so he pushed at her shirt, gliding it up her body until she lifted her head off the sand so he could remove it altogether, revealing her beautiful breasts contained in a lacy bra. He groaned, the sight one he wanted to hold in his memory for all time. He savoured the moment of seeing of her just like this, with the sun striking rays of gold across her body, her eyes glinting with sensual heat, and then he kissed her again, running his hands over her, feeling the softness of her skin, the smoothness of her hips, before he pushed at her shorts and she lifted her hips, inviting him to remove them, kicking her legs to get them off faster, until she was wearing only a pair of briefs and a bra and his own pulse was so frantic he wondered if he might be about to have a heart attack.

But wild horses were at his back, and Theresa's frantic cries were passion-soaked and urgent, so he moved his lips to her throat, then lower, flicking his tongue over her decolletage, tasting her sweet saltiness, then to her breasts. Through the fabric of her bra, he clamped his teeth around her nipple and felt a wave of masculine possessive heat when she shuddered against him, and suddenly this wasn't enough. He needed so much more.

He pushed at the fabric urgently, releasing her breasts, cupping them, holding them, feeling their weight in his hands, rubbing his hands over her puckered nipples so she arched her back in silent invitation and he brought his mouth to hers, swallowing her cries as water lapped at their feet, gently, warm, heavenly sweet.

He was urgent, there was something wild and frantic driving him, something that was completely beyond his control. He pushed at her underpants, sliding them down her legs, his breathing forced, rushed, as he stared at her then, naked beneath him, so stunning and pale against the sand, so trusting and so completely his. He groaned, because even when this felt so inevitable and *right,* on some level it felt wrong too, because she was Stavros's sister and he'd already had to make his peace with what their relationship had morphed into. Guilty or not, he surrendered, pushing out of his own clothes quickly, until he was naked before her, his arousal straining, hard and desperate, and her eyes, so round in her delicate face, fell to it, to him, staring as though she'd never seen a man before.

'Alex,' she moaned, lifting her hands, reaching for him, her cheeks pink, her lips swollen from his kisses. 'Please.'

But right as he was about to succumb, to give them both what they wanted, reality burst into his brain, well-worn habits drawing him to a stop. 'I don't have any protection,' he hissed, cursing himself for not bringing his wallet. Her cheeks grew pinker.

'It's okay,' she mumbled, so his heart slammed into his ribs and he had to stay very still to stop from immediately lowering himself to her and taking her, claiming her, as he'd wanted to do ever since she walked into his office. 'Remember, I'm on the pill,' she said. 'And I'm clean. I've been tested.'

'Me too,' he said with relief, sinking to his knees, between her legs, staring at her as though she were some kind of magical sea creature, as though this were a dream. And perhaps it was. It felt far more likely that she'd change her mind or disappear into the ocean than it was they'd actually make love, and yet she didn't make a single move to leave.

She reached for him and this time he dropped lower, so her hands curved around his arms, drawing her to him, and he kissed her again—it felt like coming home.

He couldn't stop.

His mouth ravaged hers and she whimpered, and he felt strong and powerful and terrifyingly vulnerable, brought to his knees by the strength of his need for her. She lifted her legs and wrapped them around his waist, holding him close, and though he wanted to pull back, to slow down, he couldn't. His body was independent of him, acting of its own volition, seeking hers, so he drove into her without even realising it, only her cry and his own guttural groan heralded his intrusion.

'God, Alex,' she called his name into the sky; he loved the way it sounded on her lips, heavy with passion. Her nails dragged down his back, scoring red marks, and she lifted her hips. 'Don't stop.'

'I'm not going to,' he promised, moving inside of her, feeling her tightness, the muscles gripping him as he moved, his body racked by pleasure, his needs almost overwhelming him, so he had to slow down, even when he felt as though a rhythm had overcome him. He pushed up and watched her, watched as he moved and she reacted, understood what she loved, where she was most sensitive and he teased her there, pulling out and hovering a moment before taking her again, driving her wild, to the point of incandescence, and then she was calling his name with more urgency and he was inside of her, feeling her muscles squeeze and release, losing her control completely as he swallowed her euphoric cries into his mouth, kissing her until her breath had calmed. Then, he began to move all over again, barely giving her time to recover, stoking her to new heights of desperate need, and this time, when she fell apart, he was right with her, his own release overcoming him, so he wrapped his arm around her and held her close as his body was racked with pleasure and release, and he was aware only of the sound of their breathing, of the pleasure that had exploded around them, making him feel strangely, perfectly at peace, for the first time in a long time.

His weight on her body was its own aphrodisiac. She lay beneath him, conscious of everything in that moment. Of the warmth of the sun, the lapping of the waves, the grit of the ancient sand beneath her, the hair on his chest, the strength of his frame, the heat of his skin, the hawing of his breath, the movement of his chest, *everything*. She lay perfectly still, as though it was somehow vital to feel this and relish it, to commit it to memory, to savour these feelings. As though she was aware they were hers only for a finite time. As though she knew regret would follow.

And perhaps it would, but in that moment she could only be glad, beyond words, because it felt to Tessa as though Alex had woken up an important part of her, as though he'd brought some of her back to life again.

Mortifyingly, tears dampened her eyes and she blinked furiously to clear them, but too late.

He pushed up, his body stiffening. 'Theresa?' The way he said her name made her chest heave. She bit down on her lower lip. Emotions deluged her—which was exactly what she wanted to prevent from happening.

'Yes?' She forced an overbright smile to her face, but it was belied by the salty tears filling her eyes.

'Are you okay?'

Surprised, she dragged her gaze to his face, to his grim lips, and shook her head, pressing a hand to his chest.

'I wasn't gentle,' he muttered. 'I couldn't… I was—'

'No, God, no, Alex. That was—' She bit harder into her lip. 'Honestly, perfect,' she mumbled, heat filling her cheeks as he jerked inside of her. But concern had him moving, rolling away and then standing, his back ramrod straight as he took a step towards the beach, his back to her, his attention focused on the distant horizon. Impatient with herself and desperate for him to understand, she stood, moving quickly to his side. He didn't look at her, but she could see from the set of his face that dark emotions coursed through him.

She reached for his shoulder, squeezing his bicep, so he turned to face her, his eyes loaded with self-loathing.

'Alex, I wanted that to happen.'

A muscle jerked in his jaw, as he lifted a thumb to her cheek, wiping away the tear there. 'Did you?'

'I'm not crying because I regret it.' *Though I'm sure I will.* 'I'm crying because it was so, so good and in the course of my marriage I honestly came to believe I didn't have a sexual bone in my body. I thought what we shared all those years ago was some kind of illusion. I didn't know...' She shook her head. 'The way you just made me feel, the way I feel now, truly, I have no words to express what this is like. I'm just... I've spent so long wondering if this part of me is dead, and now I know it's not. There's nothing wrong with me.'

His eyes bored into hers, his emotions unreadable. 'No, *agape.*' His voice was gruff. 'There is nothing wrong with you.'

She was shaking now as relief took over, a deep relief that sprung from the core of her doubts and worries. He moved closer, lifting his hands to either side of her face, holding her steady so he could stare at her in a way that made her feel as though her soul was on display for him to see and understand, and for some reason, despite her habit of keeping her innermost feelings secret and guarded, she didn't mind, in that moment. 'There is nothing wrong with you,' he repeated, a frown curling his mouth. 'You are passionate and sensual, beautiful and addictive.'

Addictive. Hardly. And yet, somehow, standing in that small, idyllic cove, it was easier to believe Alex's words above all else. Alex was making her feel *wonderful*, and that terrified her, because feeling great would lead her to relax, to trust him, to let herself care for him again, and Tessa couldn't risk that. She'd pull away soon. But right now it just felt so good to be close to him, naked and bathed in sunlight, the ocean wrapping around their feet with each decadent roll towards the shore.

'Just be sure to only be addicted to me between Friday and Sunday,' she said in a light-hearted tone that didn't quite ring true. But it was important to remind him—to remind them both—of the deal they'd struck.

He drew his brows together, not understanding her words, and then his face was expressionless. 'Right, the contract.'

She nodded, dislodging his hands. Or perhaps he withdrew them. Either way, the effect was the same. Her chest felt as though it were caving in. 'It makes sense,' she clarified. 'I don't want this taking over our lives.'

His eyes probed hers, and now she didn't like feeling seen, she didn't like how visible her innermost feelings were to him. 'You're really worried about that, aren't you?'

She parted her lips, a denial on her tongue, but when his eyes held hers, and their bodies were brushing, she could only be completely honest. 'Yes.' She looked up at him, hoping he'd understand. 'It has to be this way.'

The air between them crackled, tension zipping through her. She held her breath, waiting for him to say something, and in a small part of her mind she was hoping he'd argue. That he'd insist on their tearing up the contract and being married, for real, rather than the pragmatic arrangement they'd forged.

'If you say so.' It was what she wanted, and yet it left a funny feeling in her throat, as though something had lodged there and wouldn't break free. She ignored it. This was the marriage they'd agreed to—it was what they both wanted.

Tessa was an excellent chess player, and it was obvious Alex hadn't been expecting that. It was also obvious that he didn't enjoy losing. Tessa hid her smile behind a cup of tea, watching as his confident, hair-roughened fingers hovered over the pieces with what she could tell was an unusual level of uncertainty for a man like Alexandros Zacharidis. His dark eyes flicked to hers, his lips a flat line as he reached for his drink—coffee—and took a sip.

'I don't know how you drink coffee at this hour,' Tessa murmured, her eyes latched to the way his hand gripped the cup, his fingers so strong and tanned against the white ceramic, bringing back memories of his skin against hers at the beach that morning. Her heart rate doubled and her stomach squished. 'I'd be up all night.'

He replaced the cup at his side, returning his attention to the chess board. 'I'm used to it.'

'Late night chess and coffee?'

He made a growling sound. 'I haven't played chess like this in a long time.' Finally, he moved a piece—a clever move that bought him a little more time before the almost inevitable checkmate. 'Not since your brother and I used to sit up late in our dorm doing this, in fact.'

Tessa's eyes grew round in her face and something sparked inside her abdomen. 'Stavros taught me to play,' she said unevenly. 'He was very gifted, and never let me win.'

'I could say the same of you.'

She laughed softly. 'I'm not gifted. But I did have to get good, fast, playing Stav. We shared a competitive streak and a mutual hatred for losing, which meant our games were hardly quiet. My mother took to leaving the swear jar beside the board—he had a terrible vocabulary, when we played chess.'

It was Alex's turn to laugh, a throaty, guttural sound. 'I remember. Not that he lost often to me.'

'When did you start playing? You're good.'

'But not as good as you and Stavros,' he responded without ego, easing back in his chair and watching her, so she was glad she'd already formed a response to his move, and wasn't completely thrown off kilter by the intensity of his gaze. Beneath the loose kaftan she wore, and despite the balmy warmth of the night, her skin prickled with goosebumps.

'How old were you when you started playing?'

'Properly playing? Around seven.' Her smile was involuntary. 'But playing with the pieces? Much, much younger. As a girl, I used to steal into my father's study and take them for make-believe games. I would tell the most fantastical stories about the queen that was taken hostage and the army of pawns raised to save her, and the fights between the gallant knights, and finally the kings.' She shook her head. 'That was back when I still thought queens should be saved by their loyal, loving husbands.' Cynicism touched her lips. 'Your go.'

He made a noise of agreement but didn't move at all.

'Stav was the one who found me playing with the pieces. He wasn't cross, but he took them away, telling me they weren't dolls, that the set in Dad's office was actually hundreds of years old, and quite breakable. He said that if I wanted to touch them, it would need to be in a game of chess, not make-believe.'

'That sounds like Stav.'

Her heart squeezed. 'He was always an excellent rule follower.'

He shifted his fingers to the board, sliding a pawn across. She frowned at the unexpectedness of the move, momentarily distracted by his technique, which made no sense to Tessa. It was a play she hadn't seen before, and she tried to formulate his game plan, but he was too close, and his masculine fragrance was wrapping around her, so it was almost impossible to concentrate.

'And you weren't?'

'I was,' she responded, a small smile on her lips that was echoed on his.

'Stavros told how you would take the jars of Nutella from the pantry and hide them under your bed, and whenever your parents asked about it, you would shrug and say you had no idea.'

Heat coloured her cheeks. 'I was only a little girl then.'

'But you were cheeky,' he murmured.

'Yes.' Her eyes flickered to his. 'I liked to see what I could get away with.' She sipped her tea. 'And I really, really loved chocolate.'

He laughed, this time with more humour. 'And what about the sneaking out you would do? Stav said you had keys cut to the house when you were fifteen years old, so you could come and go without anyone knowing.'

Her eyes were huge. 'He *knew*?'

'I think your brother knew everything,' Alex murmured. 'He was always paying attention.'

'Yes.' She sighed heavily, missing Stavros more in that moment than she could bear.

'You were fifteen,' Alex pushed. 'Why not just ask your parents for a key?'

'Easy for you to say,' she responded quickly.

'Why?'

'You couldn't possibly understand the way they were with me.'

She bit down on her lip, pretending fascination with the chess board, when the game had momentarily lost interest for Tessa.

'They didn't want you dating,' he prompted, and when she lifted her gaze to his face he was frowning, as if trying to catch the threads of a memory. 'You had a strict curfew.'

Heat stole into her cheeks. 'Yes.'

'Why?'

She lifted her slender shoulders.

'They didn't trust you?'

'They didn't trust boys,' she said after a pause. 'And I guess they also didn't trust me.'

'Did they have a reason?'

She twisted her lips to the side. 'Not really. I was a bit naughty as a kid, but only with silly things.'

'Like jars of Nutella.'

She nodded, distracted. 'When it came to the stuff

that mattered, I think I was pretty good. I drank from time to time, at parties, but I never had a…'

'Boyfriend,' he supplied, after a pause that made Tessa wish the ground would open up and swallow her.

She nodded.

'But you went away for college. Surely by then, you could have done whatever you wanted.'

'By *then*,' she said quietly, 'I was way out of my league. I was a nineteen-year-old virgin. I was so embarrassed. I didn't want to go out with a guy and have to tell him that I hadn't even been kissed.'

Alex swore softly under his breath, and her eyes flicked to his face as realisation dawned as to what she'd just admitted.

'Just as well you like doing firsts with me,' she said with a tight smile.

He reached out and took her hand in his, lifting it to his lips. 'I do.'

It was sweet, and kind, but Tessa felt like a gauche child again. 'It wasn't just my parents. I mean, it was mostly them, but maybe that lack of confidence and experience affected me, because I never really met anyone I felt… I wasn't…' She looked at him pleadingly, hoping he understood, but he offered no help. 'I wasn't attracted to anyone. A few guys asked me out,' she said unevenly, 'but no one ever made me feel as though I couldn't bear to say no. It wasn't hard to remain a virgin, all things considered.'

His eyes narrowed thoughtfully. 'And yet, you're a very sensual woman.'

Only with you. She stayed quiet, returning her focus to the chess board and moving a piece into position.

'Why did you marry him?'

The question whipped around Tessa, startling her. She reached for her tea, sipping it, then faced him with the appearance of calm. How could she admit the truth to Alex? How could she tell him that she'd married someone partly because she'd been running from Alex, and what she'd felt with him? 'I don't really know,' she said breathily, after a moment. 'I guess I thought I loved him.'

He moved a piece without taking his eyes from her face. She didn't look down at the board immediately. 'But you didn't?'

She dropped her eyes to their game, considering her next move, then lifting her fingers to a piece and driving it across the board, leaning back with satisfaction at her manoeuvre.

She didn't know how to answer his question, and she didn't have to. A moment later he moved on, or perhaps simply changed direction.

'You haven't put on a show in years.'

Her gaze flicked to his. 'How do you know?'

'Your parents,' was his swift, flat response.

'Of course.' It wasn't as though he'd been waiting on tenterhooks for her next art show—it wasn't as though he'd ever been to one.

'How come?'

He responded to her move, but she was barely concentrating.

'I…' She sought one of her ready deflections but

none came. With Alex, she felt compelled to be honest. 'I lost my mojo for a while there. After Stavros, my work took a very dark turn,' she murmured, not admitting to Alex that his rejection of her had played a part in that. The whole world had angered her. 'Then I was a newlywed,' she said with a lift of her shoulders, oblivious to the way Alex's expression darkened, his cheeks gashed with dark colour. 'Mum and Dad were grieving. Other things took priority.' She lifted her shoulders.

'And since your divorce?'

'I'm getting there.' She lifted her shoulders. 'I'm enjoying it again.'

'I'm glad. You're very talented.'

Her eyes narrowed. 'Why would you say that?'

'Because it's true?'

'You haven't seen my art.'

'Haven't I?'

Her heart thumped into her ribs. 'I don't know.' She looked back at the board. 'I presumed not.'

'Your parents have several paintings on the walls.'

Of course. He'd been to their house. It wasn't as though he'd been to an exhibition.

'I would like to see what you've been working on lately.'

Her eyes widened and her pulse kicked up a gear. 'I'm not sure why.'

'Because you're talented,' he repeated and then, more dangerously, 'and because you're my wife.'

Possessive heat burst between them, so much more real now that they'd slept together. He stood swiftly, staring at her face for several beats before holding out his hand. 'Come with me, *agape*.'

'But the game,' she murmured, even as she placed her hand in his and stood.

'You can beat me in the morning. There are better ways to spend our night.'

CHAPTER NINE

WALKING BACK INTO Alex's stunning home in Athens felt different now, and not just because her skin was three shades darker courtesy of days stretched out by the pool. It was different because they were home, and home brought with it a crushing sense of reality. She would have been tempted to enjoy the sanctuary of his haven, where none of the real world intruded, none of the problems, none of the worries.

But that wasn't practical.

Only she hadn't banked on how pressing the real world would feel. She made a coffee and turned on her iPad and immediately it began to ping with news alerts. With a knot in her tummy, she opened them up, flicking past the fluff pieces—announcements of her marriage to Alex—and focusing on the fallout.

Jonathan, blissfully unaware that she'd remarried, courtesy of the show's sequestering of its participants, continued to divulge secrets and lies from their marriage. There was nothing of particular importance, just gossip, but Tessa's innate desire for privacy bristled at the casual way her name was being thrown around, so when Alex sauntered into the living room some time later it was to find Tessa pink-faced and jabbing at the screen, flicking an angry email to her lawyer. Surely there was a law against the press running articles without fact-checking them first? Some of the pieces were damned close to slander.

'Problem?'

Yes. She had a problem. But being back here, in Athens, reminded Tessa forcefully of who she was, of who Alex was, and the realities of their marriage. The honeymoon was over. Now they had to get on with their lives.

'No,' she clipped in response, standing and casting her iPad aside. 'I'm going to my studio to work.' She looked around for her handbag and found it on a chair nearby. 'I'll see you tonight.'

He watched her go without evincing a single emotion. She was a free agent. If she wanted to work, of course she could. He had plans to return to the office himself, though he hadn't been planning to rush in there today. In fact, there were many other things he thought he might enjoy doing far, far more. But Tessa had been withdrawing from him ever since they'd left Epíneio. She'd read her book on the boat, made polite small talk only when absolutely necessary, and then sat silently during the car trip back to his place.

He hadn't pushed her.

Their situation was complex and the marriage new. They were both navigating it as best they could.

With a frown, he moved absentmindedly to the sofa,

his hand brushing the back, where she'd been sitting, before his eyes landed on the iPad, a moment before the screen went black. But he'd seen it first—the picture of her and Jonathan with a splashy tabloid heading. Reaching for the device, he swiped it open and read the article with grimly held lips.

So her ex-husband was still spewing his disgusting nonsense? Just as Tessa had feared he would.

And their marriage hadn't stopped the stories from leaking into the headlines. His first thought was of Tessa, but very quickly his mind shifted to her father, to the plan she'd had to save her parents from any further pain caused by her idiot ex.

This wasn't working. Would it ever have worked? And if not, why had he agreed?

Then again, a quick Google search showed that the only place Jonathan's indiscreet blather landed was in the most low-rent tabloids. No broadsheet masthead was remotely interested in his troublemaking stories. Their marriage had more coverage, simply because it had invigorated share prices for both companies as news of a corporate merger gained steam.

And?

He rubbed a hand over the back of his neck, staring into space as he considered that. Orion was getting older, and his heart was failing. Since Stavros's death he'd returned to the role of CEO, but surely alleviating those pressures would be beneficial?

Would he agree to hand the reins over to Alex? And would Tessa think he was taking on too much, given the nature of their marriage?

He replaced the iPad with a growing sense of unease. The straight lines he'd planned to hold in place seemed to be starting to wobble, but Alex simply wouldn't let them. He expelled a long, slow breath, retaking a grip on reality. Nothing had changed since that morning. They were married, in a very specific kind of marriage, and her issues were still there, just as they had been before.

It was just as they'd agreed.

He showered quickly and left for the office, seeking normality and escape from the direction of his thoughts.

Tessa painted with anger. She painted with grief. But she also painted beauty and pain and the inescapable presence of both in life, the euphoria of bliss shadowed by the threat of loss. She painted Epíneio, the shoreline, with white sand beaches and frangipani trees casting a telltale shadow. It was only when looking closely that one could see the dark depth of those shadows, the ominous promise of their presence.

She painted, the light in her studio perfect, the sun streaming in through the large windows of the disused fire station she shared with two other artists, and she worked tirelessly, ignoring the painting hanging to her left, the pair of eyes staring back at her that were now as familiar to her as her own had been.

She painted under Alex's gaze, the painting she'd done in the week after they slept together, when he'd filled her mind and heart and soul and she'd yearned for him, and ached for him, and had wanted a piece of him even though she could never have him.

She wasn't sure why she'd kept the painting all these years.

It wasn't her usual thing.

She loved landscapes and still life. But his face had taken shape and she'd sculpted his features onto the canvas brushstroke by brushstroke, particularly proud of the cynical mockery she'd captured in his eyes, the derisive curl of his lips. It was how she'd always wanted to remember him—scathing. Hurtful. Because she'd known she could never forget.

Yet here she was, blissfully sinking back into a state of unawarness, allowing herself to delight in his company, to delight in him.

She dropped her head forward, into her hands, and moaned. Everything had seemed so simple, but it wasn't, and, no matter how determined she was to maintain their contractual agreement, she couldn't change the fact that he'd become a part of her all over again.

Tessa painted until the light was dim and her hand cramping, but some time after eight she packed up, diligently cleaning her brushes, sealing her paints, wiping her work surface and locking up the shared studio space, moving slowly, because in the back of her mind was a sense of dread at the evening ahead.

In Epíneio, they'd become close. Sleeping together, swimming, playing chess. The past had ceased to matter. But here, it was all around her, and the weight of that truth pressed into her like concrete.

She couldn't pretend this was simple, she couldn't pretend it was safe. Tessa had to keep her wits about her.

He was in the kitchen when she walked through the door, and the moment their eyes met her heart began to skitter and roll.

'Hi.' A deep, throaty greeting that made her stomach drop to her toes.

Her hands clasped more tightly around her bag. 'Hi.' Her own voice was breathy, hoarse from misuse. She cleared her throat.

'How are you?'

'Fine.' She cleared her throat again.

'I was just about to order dinner. What do you feel like?'

Panic skittled through her. She couldn't do this. She couldn't pretend everything was fine. It wasn't. Suddenly her head was swimming—with worries about her dad, anger at Jonathan, and most of all confusion about the man she'd married, the man who'd broken her heart, the only man she'd ever loved.

'Nothing. I'm not hungry. I—' she looked anxiously towards the hallway '—I'm going to catch up on emails in my room. Goodnight, Alex.'

He watched her walk away with a groaning sense of impatience. *My room. Goodnight, Alex.* Was she kidding? They'd spent five days living in each other's pockets on Epíneio and now she wanted to go back to separate bedrooms? To sex on weekends, as she'd originally suggested? Before he could stop himself, he began to move after her. 'Wait a second.'

Her shoulders slumped, and if he'd been thinking straight, that would have been enough to make Alex pause, but his own emotions were crowding him, so it was almost impossible to comprehend hers.

'Yes?' Her voice was quiet, soft.

His gut twisted. 'You are running away from me,' he said simply, because there was nothing else he could say. He just wanted her to confirm it. No, he wanted her to explain it, too.

'I'm just going to my room,' she said softly.

'Why?' he pushed.

Her eyes lanced him and then dropped away. The turmoil in them was too much to bear. He ached for her. The Jonathan media storm might have seemed like nonsense to him, but to Tessa it was obviously painful. But didn't she understand, he could fix this? He could fix it by holding her close, by making love to her, by getting his legal team involved with the newspapers running the baseless stories. He could fix everything if she'd let him.

'I need to be alone,' she replied quietly.

'But you are not alone,' he insisted, moving closer, gratified when she stood her ground rather than moving back. 'I'm right here, and I can help you.'

She bristled. 'I don't want help.'

'Why not?'

She looked up at him, anguish in her face. 'Because this is my problem.'

'And I'm your husband.'

'But not really,' she pointed out quickly. 'You were so, so kind to marry me, and at the time I really thought our marriage would fix everything, but it didn't, and I just—need to think.'

Something shifted at his side. He felt as though he'd been punched, hard, right in the gut. 'Are you saying you want a divorce?'

Her skin paled. 'No.' She shook her head for emphasis. 'That would make everything worse. Unless you want a divorce, in which case of course I'll agree.'

He wondered at the anger writhing inside his chest. 'No,' he said slowly. 'I want to be married to you. Your father's health situation has not changed, has it?'

She shook her head.

'Then we stick to our agreement,' he said quietly.

'Exactly.' She pressed a hand to his chest as if in triumph. 'And this *is* what we agreed, remember? Through the week, we keep to ourselves. Weekends are…different.'

He was more irritated than he should have been. 'Right, on weekends we can have sex.' He said it to provoke her. He said it because he was mad, and he hated himself for that, because dealing with his feelings was clearly the last thing she needed. But hell, she was pushing him away right when he wanted to comfort her, and Alex wasn't one to be told what to do and where to be. She needed him. She needed comfort.

Or did she need space, just as she was saying?

'Yes,' she agreed without meeting his eyes. 'Fine. But right now I want to go to my room and have a bath, and then go to bed,' she admitted, her voice quivering, so all the anger he'd been feeling, the frustration, disappeared on a wave of concern.

'Okay,' he said after a loaded pause, surprising himself with his capitulation. But Tessa was telling him what she needed; he'd be a fool not to listen. 'That makes sense. Why don't you go and run the bath and I'll bring you a glass of wine in ten minutes?'

Her eyes clung to his and the sight of tears sparkling on her lashes made him want to pull her towards him again, to wrap her up in a big hug and promise her everything was going to be okay. She didn't deserve any of this. Just as they'd come together in grief on the night of Stav's funeral, he wanted to make love to her now, to blot out her pain, to make her feel better. He wanted to make love to her because it was the *right* thing to do, because they both needed it, but he took a step backwards, because he wasn't his father and she wasn't his mother and they were capable of making decisions in their marriage that were rational and calm.

'Go on,' he said gruffly, knowing he'd change his mind if she lingered.

In the bath, she gave in to the tears that had been threatening since that morning.

Finally alone, she let them slide down her face without thinking they were a form of weakness, without worrying she was betraying herself in some vital way. It was okay to be sad. It was okay to feel completely sideswiped by the news of today.

Footsteps in the bedroom outside had her dipping her hands in the bathwater and lifting it to her face, splashing her eyes with the bubble-filled water so the telltale sign of tears wouldn't be so apparent.

He knocked on the door and waited, and the small gesture did all sorts of things to her.

'Come in.'

He held out the glass of wine, offering it to her from a safe distance.

'Thank you,' she murmured, curving her fingers around it.

'Want me to go?' he asked, with no pressure, no expectation.

The problem was, she wanted him to stay, which was exactly why she needed him to leave. She couldn't let herself go down this path. 'Please,' she said without meeting his eyes, so she didn't see the way his lips compressed at the single word.

'I'll be downstairs if you need me.'

He was doing everything right: giving her space, respecting her boundaries. So why did she feel so utterly rubbish when she was, once again, alone?

CHAPTER TEN

THOUGH TESSA COULD scarcely believe it, the next day things launched from bad to worse. A friend texted her the headlines: *Heiress Ice Queen*. An article followed full of drama and misinformation, quoting a lengthy conversation Jonathan had had with a one-hit-wonder pop star also residing in the Celebrity House, in which he'd cried his heart out about his unfeeling ex-wife, relaying minute details of their marriage, as well as many, many points of fiction. She read it with a strange sense that she was choking.

'Good morn...' The greeting died on Alex's lips when he saw her face. 'Theresa?'

She nodded, numb, unable to speak, then pulled her phone from her pocket, flicked it to life and handed it to him, the offending article on the screen. 'It's never going to stop, is it?'

She watched him at first, but after a moment the look on his face was too much to bear. She turned her back, bracing her palms on the counter, staring out at his stunning infinity pool and, beyond it, Athens.

'This guy is a pig,' Alex muttered with cold derision.

Tessa flinched. 'Yes, but he's a pig that's going to keep squealing for the rest of my life,' she said softly, the reality of that driving any brightness from her mind. 'I made a mistake when I married him, I know that, but I am going to have to keep paying for that mistake for a very long time.'

Behind her, Alex stiffened. Not if he could help it. This had gone on long enough. From the brief details he'd gathered from Theresa, their marriage had been borderline abusive. Oh, Jonathan might not have hit her, but he was coercive and a bully, and had undermined her at every opportunity. Emotional abuse was still a torment, and he was continuing to chip away at her. To see beautiful, intelligent, funny Theresa cowered by her ex-husband's indiscretion made him want to punch something. It sure as hell made him want to wrap her in cotton wool.

But hadn't she had enough of that?

Hell. He dragged a hand through his hair, two sides of Alexandros at war within him. His first instinct was to protect her, to make her feel safe and happy, and he could think of one sure-fire way to do that. But his second instinct was to give her the space to work this out for herself, because he knew that was important to her, and her independence would be more meaningful if she found her way there on her own. She'd been protected all her life—over-protected—and she'd hated it. Wouldn't she come to resent him if he tried to coddle her? Wouldn't she hate it, and possibly him, if he got involved?

He knew the second instinct was what he should listen to, but maybe there was a way to do both?

'Let's go back to Epíneio,' he said, his voice firmly insistent.

She turned to face him, eyes widened, and he knew then he'd found the right option. It was obvious that she was tempted. 'That won't solve anything.'

'Won't it?'

She shook her head sadly. 'This is my life now.'

'That's the point.' Screw it. He closed the distance between them and lifted her up, sitting her on the edge of the kitchen bench so he could stand between her legs, their gazes level. 'It's only your life if you let it be. On Epíneio, did he enter your head, *at all*?'

She frowned, eyes searching his.

He pushed on, regardless of the fact she hadn't answered. 'He is going to try to spin out the secrets of your marriage—'

'And lies,' she interjected hotly.

'Yes,' he conceded. 'For as long as there's commercial value in him doing so. But no one who knows you will take any notice. He's providing salacious gossip, it's true—'

'And I'm at the heart of it,' she moaned, shaking her head softly.

'Which is frustrating,' he was quick to agree, because the last thing she needed was to have her feelings rendered invalid. 'But you are a much better person than him. Every lie he tells, every story he sells, that hits the bottom-feeding tabloids, and every day that you stay silent, speaks volumes about his character—and yours. You have so much integrity, Theresa, whereas I doubt he even knows how to spell the word.'

She blinked slowly, then focused on a point over his shoulder. He wasn't getting through to her.

'You married me for two reasons. One of them was to drown out his stories with news of your own. The other was for your father.'

Her eyes met his and she nodded slowly.

'Every day that your father believes our marriage to be real, and us to be happy, is a gift to him.' Alex leaned closer, truth and wisdom in his eyes. 'But there is a third reason perhaps you weren't aware of. Let's call it a silver lining.'

'Oh?' she whispered. 'What's that?'

'On Epíneio you are happy, and you deserve that. Isn't the best revenge living well?'

She bit down on her lip. He was right, but what about the inherent risks of being close to him? On Epíneio she was in the most danger of forgetting their boundaries, of imagining this marriage to be real, of hoping it might morph into everything she'd ever wanted.

'Let's go there, today. Let me help you forget.' He expelled a sharp breath. 'You wanted to change the narrative? So change it here.' He pressed a finger between her breasts, feeling the steady thumping of her heart. 'Free yourself from him. As long as he can upset you, he wins.'

'It's not just me. It's my parents, my friends, and now it's you.'

'Me?'

'It's anyone who knows me, who is embarrassed by this—'

'I'm not embarrassed.' He moved closer, pressing his lips to her forehead, so angry that she could feel any of these things. 'I don't give a— I don't care what he says about you. I know you, the real you. And anyone else who does will see this for what it is.'

He felt her sharp intake of breath.

'His stories *will* lose currency. At some point the media will move on, and his fifteen seconds of fame will be at an end. Or he'll be married and divorced from someone else he's trying to exploit.' He shrugged, staying close to her. 'All you can control is how you respond to his behaviour. Come away with me. Forget him.' And then he kissed her, to show her how easy this could be, and how right it felt. He told himself this was the best, smartest option, that she was his wife, and it was his duty to help her, even as he felt something shift between them, something he couldn't explain.

Perhaps she felt it too, because she pulled away warily. 'This doesn't change anything,' she said, curling her fingers in his shirt. 'Our marriage isn't real, Alex.'

'I know that.' His voice emerged clipped and cold now, as if pushing away the tenderness he'd just shown, in a moment of weakness. 'We both know the deal.'

'Do we?' She scanned his face. 'Because the last thing I want is to get involved with anyone. Emotionally, I mean.' Pink darkened her cheeks. 'I can't give you more than this,' she whispered. 'I won't.'

'Then it's just as well I'm not asking for more,' he

said simply, honestly, even when a stitch formed in his side. 'Neither of us wants a relationship.'

She bit down on her lip. 'How do we make sure we remember that?'

'By not falling in love,' he said, as though it were the simplest thing in the world.

'That's why I want to limit our time together...'

'Let me make you this promise, *agape*,' he said, wanting to assuage her concerns. 'It doesn't matter how much time we spend together, or how often we sleep together. I will not fall in love with you, and I will make sure you don't fall in love with me. I don't want a real marriage,' he said darkly. 'I just want to enjoy what works between us. Trust me.'

Three hours later, on the beach of Epíneio, it was impossible to question his logic. All her problems still existed, but they felt so far away, and here, on this stunning island floating in the middle of the Aegean, she could *breathe*. 'Perhaps there's something to be said for running away after all,' she said with a half-smile for the man who'd rolled up his sleeves and waded into the madness of her life, to hell with the consequences.

'Definitely.' He drew her closer, one arm around her shoulders, holding her against his side in a gesture of friendship and support. At least, that was what it was supposed to be, but the second they connected, heat exploded inside her, and her body softened against him, wordlessly inviting him closer, conveying her need for him. It was a need he could stir so easily! She knew better than to try tamping down on her desire, but she held her resolution close to her heart: when they were back in Athens, she'd reinstate the rules they'd agree to. This was an aberration. A moment out of time, exempt from their agreement, because Jonathan had been such a monumental jerk. Yes, they were cheating, but it was justified.

Convinced enough to let go of her control, just a little, she tilted her face to his, and when he kissed her she smiled against his mouth, feeling, for a moment, as though everything was exactly as it was supposed to be. For the first time in years, she relaxed—in the midst of the storm that was her life, here in this haven, with Alexandros at her side, she was happier than she'd been in a long time.

He waited until she was asleep before leaving the bed, moving to the door of the room and hesitating a moment, studying her from guarded eyes, weighing up what he intended to do before he slipped from the room completely.

Alex was not a man to second-guess his instincts, and ever since yesterday morning he'd known one thing for certain: he could not sit by and allow Tessa to be her ex-husband's punching bag.

Though he thought of Epíneio as his haven from the frenetic pace of his real life, he wasn't able to escape it completely, and the office here reflected that. It was a state-of-the-art space, with two side-by-side computer screens, and all the technology he required to be able to function at his level without interruption.

He stepped inside with determination, moving towards his desk and flicking the computers to life as he reached for his phone and dialled his office, only one person in mind that he could trust with this. 'Get me Berringer,' he said, without preamble.

'Yes, sir, of course.' His assistant put him through immediately, despite the lateness of the hour, and Berringer answered on the third ring. In the background there was the clinking of glasses, the sound of laughter.

'You're busy?' he prompted.

'I have friends for dinner, it's not important,' Berringer said.

Alex pushed back in his chair. He didn't like to eat into his staff's private lives, and yet he paid well above the average.

'I have time, sir. What is it?' There was the clicking of a door, and then the noise dulled.

'This won't take long.' Alex pushed aside his qualms about the timing of his call. He had to know this matter was dealt with. 'I need you to do something for me. Delegate, if necessary, but it must be handled.'

He proceeded to outline the list he'd come up with: threaten the television network with a lawsuit for slander, threaten Jonathan's lawyer with the same, regardless of the fact he was in the *Celebrity Housemates* complex and sequestered from communication, and include a promise for more detailed litigation if Jonathan didn't submit to a retroactive confidentiality clause. Alex had no idea if it would work. God knew he had the teeth to pursue Jonathan through all the courts in Europe, but did Theresa have the stomach for that?

He suspected not.

The last thing she wanted was more drama and attention on her private life, and if there was a big legal bust-up it would lead to that. So he had to hope the threats would be sufficient. And if they weren't? Would he go against her wishes and use his deep pockets to simply make this problem go away?

He closed his eyes and saw her face, the hurt there as she'd read the article, the hauntedness around her eyes and lips, the sense of betrayal, and he knew that, yes, he would do anything he could in order to relieve her pain. For Stavros, he had to. He owed his best friend that much, at least.

For no reason that he could think of, he loaded up the latest article and began to read, phone tucked under his ear. Just as with the first time, his blood pressure went through the roof, until he could take it no longer and jackknifed to standing, stalking across the room to the window and staring out at it, his body very still. The ocean was dark tonight, the moon submerged by thick clouds, so even the trees were lost in the darkness. It suited his mood to look out and see darkness. And yet, at just that moment, the clouds parted, and a pure beam of moonlight split through, casting the ground in silvery light. He braced his hip against the window frame, staring out at the ocean, a frown marring his face. Darkness and light. Black night and moonlight. Would each be as beautiful without the other?

'I want to show you something.'

She jolted her gaze to him, the X-rated nature of her thoughts surely written all over her expression as her husband stepped onto the pool deck. She flicked some water over her knees, waiting for him to elaborate.

'Come with me.'

She lifted a single brow but stood, her knees a little unsteady, and her awareness of Alex only grew when he reached down and laced their fingers together as naturally as if they were truly a couple.

He guided her away from the house, and down a winding, gravel path, to a small building she hadn't seen before.

'What is it?'

The walls were whitewashed, the roof terracotta, and a large barn door made of glass was painted in peeling turquoise paint. He swished it open, and then gestured for her to step inside. She did so, with a small frown, onto a painted concrete floor.

'Your studio, if you want it to be.'

Her eyes widened as she turned to look at him, and a thousand things flashed through her mind. Pleasure, because this was so thoughtful. Danger, because it was thoughtful, and if she wasn't careful she might read something into that, and excitement, because the need to paint only intensified when she was here.

'I have an office inside,' he pointed out. 'It only makes sense for you to have a studio.'

'That's so kind, Alex. I really—I'm blown away. Thank you.' Her voice cracked so she cleared her throat, moving deeper into the space and admiring the light streaming in through the wide doors, and then the view of the ocean she could see from the windows on the side. 'I love it.'

'I'm glad.' His voice was cool, with no hint of emotion. She stifled a sigh. On the face of it, this seemed like a thoughtful gesture, but she'd be reading more into it if she allowed that to mean anything. More likely, it was just Alex's practical brain taking over, thinking of ways she could be kept busy while on the island, so he could work guilt-free.

That dose of reality was essential, but it did take the shine off things, just a little.

When she turned back to him, her smile didn't reach her eyes. 'I'll organise some equipment when we're next in Athens.'

He nodded his agreement, waiting by the door.

'You woke early,' she murmured as they made their way back towards the house.

'Yes.'

'I thought this was your haven, where you come to relax?'

'I am relaxed.' He shrugged, his frame as rigid as a brick wall.

She threw him a sidelong glance. 'Then why get out of bed in the small hours of the morning?'

'Actually, I worked through the night.'

She blinked. 'You did?'

'You fell asleep, and my mind was racing, so I went into my office.'

She grimaced. 'I hardly slept the night before that.' She frowned. 'Actually, I'd barely slept since leaving Epíneio, but here, something about the sea breeze and the rolling waves... I could fall asleep right now.'

'Would you like me to tuck you into bed?' he offered, and her pulse kicked up a gear.

She needed boundaries…almost as much as she needed him. She nodded slowly, fatalistically, because how could she resist?

The temptation to stay in bed all day was hard to ignore, but he forced himself to, stretching and pulling away from Tessa's naked body even when he wanted to stay with one arm clamped around her waist, holding her to him.

Beyond her window, the ocean glistened, and the sky was a brilliant blue. An idea bubbled in his veins, and he didn't stop to question the wisdom of it, just as he hadn't the suggestion to come to Epíneio, nor to offer her the old guest house as a studio.

'How'd you like to hit the water?'

'A swim?' she murmured.

'Eventually. I was thinking a jet ski first.'

Her smile was spontaneous and mesmerising. 'I'd like that.' She nodded. 'I'd like it a lot.'

CHAPTER ELEVEN

HER BODY WAS pressed close to his as he surfed the coastline, tracing the outline of the island from the water, showing her hollowed-out caves dug into the cliff face, and the little stone cottages that his staff used when they were on the island, as well as grapevines that yielded just enough fruit to make a small pressing of wine, and the nimble mountain goats that had graduated to the edge of a cliff now, and were lazily chomping their way through wildflowers. Everything about the island fascinated her, and the man in front of her, whose body she had her arms tightly wound around, fascinated her most of all.

There was danger in that sentiment—it was the opposite of how she should feel—but there was something about Alex that made her want to stop time and devour him. To understand him completely—everything about him—even when she knew him on an instinctive level that defied explanation.

Jet skiing was wonderful, but when they returned to the house Alex said he had work to do, and disappeared abruptly, leaving her alone. She told herself she was glad, that their time together had to be carefully balanced, or there would be too much danger. She read for a while, then wandered into what would become her studio and imagined how she'd lay out the furniture, then, as the sun started to become almost too much, she stripped down to her bathers and stood on the edge of the pool, toes curled over the coping, eyes chasing the ripples of the water. She counted to ten, breathed in deeply then dived in, cracking beneath the surface and spearing through the water, holding her breath all the way to the other side, before pushing up and resting her arms on the edge of the pool.

'Mind if I join you?'

She bit back a smile as she turned to see Alex crouching on the side of the pool, his fingertips caressing the water.

'It's your pool.' She shrugged, hiding the fact that she wanted him to join her almost more than anything.

His eyes were lightly mocking, as though he understood the stand she was taking. He stood, eyes still on her as he stripped out of his shirt, leaving him standing in just a pair of boardshorts that did little to hide the muscular nature of his body. Her mouth felt as acrid as the desert as he walked around the pool, closer to her, his every step an inducement, a temptation, a fascination, so that by the time he'd reached her the air in her lungs seemed to crackle.

He stood directly in front of her, his hair-roughened legs and strong calves so close she had an irrational urge to pull herself out of the water and press her lips to his flesh there. Thankfully, before she could indulge that craving, he lifted his arms over his head and dived in, his body a study of strength and elegance as he swam to the other end of the pool easily. When he was halfway there she could no longer fight her body's cravings and she gave chase, moving beneath the water to follow him stealthily, eyes scanning to find him. When he changed direction she followed, no longer pursuing him beneath the water but splashing on top of it, moving faster, laughing as she got close and he slipped away, changing direction again, spinning easily in the water, his far more powerful stroke no match for hers. So when she caught him, finally, she suspected it was because he'd allowed it, but that didn't make the success any less sweet. Her fingers curved around his bicep, and he laughed, drawing her closer, their arms tangling as they splashed in the water. He was so much stronger, and yet he let himself be caught and tamed, let her body wrap around his, until she was breathless from laughing and the exertion, in his arms, legs wrapped around his waist, so close to him she felt as though they were one person.

'Hi.' She smiled, all rules momentarily pushed from her mind by the pleasure of this moment. Her lashes were clumped from the water and her dark hair fell like silk down her back.

'Hi.' He grinned back, his handsome face knocking the air completely from her lungs.

The sunset was stunning, and she was aware of it in her peripheral vision, but mostly she was aware of the man in front of her, of how perfectly they fitted together, and of how much she liked being here with him, like this.

Before the idea could terrify her, and make her pull away from him, he shifted, kissing her—wet, urgent, important kisses that spoke of time wasted and imperative needs. Breathless, she kissed him back, and as he steered them through the water she didn't argue, but let him direct them to the wide pool steps, lifting her bottom onto the edge of one so that he could kiss her properly, his body dominating easily, hers surrendering to his completely. It was a magical night, from the colour of the sky to the perfection of his possession. He peeled her bathing costume off easily, then dispensed with his own, tossing both onto the pool tiles before kissing her again, slowly at first, and then with desperate need, until she was a quivering mess in his arms. When he parted her legs and moved between them she bit down on her lip so hard she almost drew blood, holding her breath until he thrust into her, and her muscles squeezed him in welcome abandon.

They were unified by passion and need, each moving with the same desperate haste, she writhing to be closer to him, he rolling his hips until she was incandescent, the water lapping around them creating waves that rivalled the ocean's, until finally they exploded in a shared, redefining moment, clinging to one another as though that was the only way they could make sense of what they were doing.

When he pulled away a little, so he could look down at her, she saw the dark slash of colour on his cheeks and felt a rush of female power to know that for all he could drive her wild, she did the exact same to him. It was a shot of confidence and a balm to her traumatised soul. She pressed a palm to his chest, smiling contentedly when she felt the strong racing of his heart.

In the space of a week, she'd gone from thinking of herself as entirely sexless to suspecting she might actually be a little bit of a sex goddess. The thought made her laugh softly beneath her breath, earning a cocked brow from Alex.

'Something funny, Mrs Zacharidis?'

Her heart stammered and air was suddenly in short supply. 'I…'

Mrs Zacharidis. How ridiculous that it had only just hit her fully: they were married. Man and wife, for the rest of her life.

Her gaze dropped to the water beneath them as emotions too strong to interpret began to pull on her. 'I was just thinking that a week ago I would have said I didn't have a sexual bone in my body,' she said with a small shrug.

'You hadn't had the opportunity to get to know yourself properly.'

'No, I suppose not.' She lifted her face to his. 'Except for that one night, when I was just too grief-filled to realise that what we'd shared was…' She stalled, not sure she could put into words what she thought about that night, nor what it had come to mean to her during her marriage.

'Yes?'

Perfect. She couldn't admit that. It hadn't been perfect…it had been a lie. Just as this was a lie. Not the sex, though. But beyond that? Her heart beat harder, faster, more urgently, demanding that she listen.

Alex had rejected her four years earlier, and despite the fact they'd only spent one night together, it had broken her. His words had shattered her in two. She'd married Jonathan in the stupid hope that she could start to feel normal again, but it had failed, because Alex had always been there, larger than life, in her mind, her memories, her studio, and her heart.

Instinctively she shied away from any deeper self-analysis, because it would be too catastrophic if she was to start thinking she'd done something stupid and fallen in love with him. Even the idea had her stiffening, breaking away, putting space between them, physically and, she hoped, emotionally.

It was one of the things she'd come to love most about being on the island with Alex. Walking aimlessly, directionless, along his private beaches, sand warm beneath their toes, water lapping at their feet, and the sun, half-concealed by the horizon now, spread a blanket of gold from it to them, so it seemed as though there was something magical in the air. When they walked it was easy to talk, or to simply be silent, side by side, and it was natural for his hand to reach down and grab hers, to lace their fingers together in a small yet intimate contact that did funny things to her heart.

'There's something I'd like to discuss with you.'

His tone of voice was flattened of emotion but the formality of his statement had her slowing. 'Oh?'

'Your father's company cannot keep running with him at the helm.'

Oh. Relief began to throb inside her chest.

'He's not well, and there's too much pressure on him.'

'His VP—'

'Is not a man I respect,' Alex dismissed swiftly. 'And nor does your father, clearly, or he'd have handed over the reins a long time ago.'

That was a fair point.

'You know Dad. He's a control freak.'

'I understand that,' Alex said with a lift of his shoulders. 'He owes it to his shareholders—and himself—to protect his legacy.'

'What are you suggesting?'

'That I buy into the company and take over as CEO.'

Her jaw dropped. 'You're kidding?'

'You don't like the idea?'

She tucked a stray strand of hair behind her ear. 'It's not that.' She struggled to think. 'It's just, you have your own enormous business to run.'

'I can do both.'

Which would leave them very little time to share. The thought was a red herring but she pushed it away nervously, only to have a far less pleasant one enter her head. Was he doing this to avoid her? Was he already getting bored of her? Regretting this? She looked away.

'If that's the case, then you should speak to Dad. It's nothing to do with me.'

He made a noise of impatience. 'It has everything

to do with you. You're a major shareholder, for a start, and secondly...'

But he didn't finish, so she turned to look at him, only to find he'd stopped walking and was staring into the ocean, his expression brooding.

'Secondly?' she prompted, surprised at the sharp tone in her voice.

He began to walk once more, catching up to her. 'I don't want you to think it's why I married you,' he said finally. 'There's financial advantage in this for me.'

'You have enough money,' she pointed out.

'Yes.'

'And I know why you married me.' Something sat hard in her throat. She looked away. 'I get where you're coming from. You want to help Dad. I'm okay with that, of course.'

And she was, for the most part. But the undercurrent to every conversation was the sense that they were becoming more and more entwined, and that it spelled danger for Tessa. She couldn't think of Alex without a strange sensation stealing through her heart.

They walked in silence for a while, just the waves bringing soft, shushing sounds towards them, and the night birds beginning to sing their lovely, high-pitched songs, so Tessa breathed in deeply then exhaled.

'How come you got involved in shipping?' she asked thoughtfully as the sun dipped completely behind the ocean, slipping to the other side of the world.

'I had an opportunity, right out of college. I didn't want to take over my father's company.' A muscle jerked in his jaw, so she felt the emotion behind his simple admission. 'So I raised as much capital as I could, as quickly as I could—your parents were early investors, did you know that?'

She shook her head.

'And then I bought a small line of boats.'

'Which you've somehow turned into all this.'

He lifted his shoulders. 'Global logistics boomed right as I moved into it.'

'If I didn't know you better, I'd say you were being modest.'

He laughed. 'Fine, I have good instincts, and I worked hard. I worked very hard. I was determined to make a name for myself, outside of my father's money.'

'Why?'

His pace slowed, ever so slightly. 'Isn't that normal?'

She shook her head slowly. 'I don't think so. You come from old money. Your father inherited his parents' business and so on and so forth. To strike out on your own—'

'I'm Chairman of my father's company.'

'But you still refer to it as your father's company.'

'He only died six months ago.'

Sympathy shifted through her. 'I know.' She moved closer, pulling her hand free so she could put it around his waist instead, needing full body contact to convey the depth of her sympathy. 'It was so sudden.'

'Yes.' He dropped a kiss on the top of her head and brought his arm around to drape over her shoulders. Something clicked into place inside her, so despite the heaviness of their conversation, she was utterly at ease.

'But it will take me a while—if ever—to stop thinking of those businesses as his.'

'Before he—before you lost him, you were still hands-off with those companies. Why?'

'Haven't I already answered that?'

She frowned. 'I don't think so.'

He laughed, but it was a sound without humour. 'You're too damned perceptive.'

'I just have a feeling there's more to it.'

'And what gives you that feeling?'

'I can't explain it. I just…know you.' Their eyes met and her heart zinged with the power of a full-blown electrical storm. Her knees went weak. She looked away, and when he spoke his voice was distant, cool.

'I loved my father, naturally. I admired him a great deal. He was strong and smart and fiercely determined. But I also hated him, Theresa.'

She jerked her face to his.

'My childhood was spent watching him obliterate my mother's sense of self, watching them argue like cats and dogs, watching her spiral further and further into misery, and my father never doing anything to help her. I don't know why. Ego, perhaps? She needed help, and instead he fought with her, again and again. Their divorce should have liberated her from the situation, but by then she was destroyed. Their marriage had taken its toll.' He paused, swallowing and looking out to sea. 'When she died, a part of me broke off and went with her. I knew I could never forgive him. For all the ways he treated her in their marriage, and for how he was with her after. She killed herself, but in many ways he killed her too.'

Tessa's eyes closed, her lashes hiding the tears that were forming.

'The idea of working with him, enriching his companies further, was anathema to me. He was my father, and I loved him, but it was not an easy relationship, and when he died I mourned more than just him; I felt as though I was losing her all over again, too. We never spoke about her. We never spoke about their fights, their marriage. All I knew was that she'd loved him, violently, and that love had killed her.' He turned back to face Tessa, his lips twisting in a cynical grimace.

She nuzzled closer, pressing her head against his chest, slowing them to a stop and just standing there, two people embracing on the shoreline as the stars began to shine.

'And so you see love as bad?' she murmured.

'Yes.' His smile was mocking. 'I don't see any upside to it. You open yourself up to someone, and what for? I'm happy as I am.'

Her throat worked overtime as she swallowed hard, trying to remove the taste of bitterness. 'I'm sorry for what you've been through. I'm sorry for your mother.'

'I wanted to save her, Theresa. I wanted to, so badly, but I was too young, and her needs were so difficult to grasp. I didn't know how...' He growled, his frustration obvious.

Sympathy washed through Tessa, but so did comprehension, in equal measure. 'And so you saved me instead,' she murmured as a pang of guilt tightened her chest. Because unconsciously she'd presented him with a situation he could never say 'no' to.

She'd come to him as a woman in distress, a woman who'd been made miserable in her marriage, who'd been emotionally manipulated and abused to the point she'd forgotten who she was and had certainly lost the waypoint to her inner strength. But Alex hadn't been prepared to let history repeat itself, and so he'd stepped in, to save the day. He wasn't a child any longer, but a grown man, perfectly able to be the saviour.

It all made perfect sense, and his actions were no less honourable, but she felt a strange heaviness resting in her chest all of a sudden, and she pulled away from him, forcing a smile to her face. 'Let's go back and have dinner. I'm starving.'

CHAPTER TWELVE

THE ISLAND WAS a haven, but not from Tessa's thoughts. The longer they remained, the harder it was to fight the inner knowledge she was wrestling with, the love that was taking hold of her, that scared the hell out of her, because of how vulnerable that love would make her. Neither of them wanted a marriage built on love, but she could no longer deny to herself the feelings that were stirring through her, feelings she'd always had for Alex. Why else would his rejection have hurt so damned much?

If she told him how she felt, it would be an unbearable burden.

She knew what he feared most in the world; she knew how he felt about love.

She'd heard the rich emotion in his voice when he'd spoken of his parents' marriage, of his mother's love for his father, and how that love had been her downfall. What would his protective instincts do if she told him—or even just showed him—her love?

A lump formed in her throat as she stared out at the

early morning coastline, the trees almost silver in the cool morning light.

He could *never* know the truth.

She wasn't aware of Alex's approach, but the fragrance of coffee curled around her and she cast a look over her shoulder, her heart giving an enormous jump at the sight of him, dressed in a suit now—like the Alex he'd been on the day she'd proposed this marriage.

'You're a little overdressed for our island vibe,' she observed with a sideways tilt of her head.

His smile was like warm honey on her spine, and she shivered, taking the coffee with a grateful smile that felt tight on her lips.

'I have meetings in Athens today.'

'Ah.' Another shiver, this time shaped by the idea of the city. It wasn't geographically far, but at the same time it was a million miles away from Epíneio.

He crouched beside her, tailored trousers straining across his haunches, drawing her gaze, stirring hunger in the pit of her stomach. She sipped her coffee, closing her eyes as the taste assaulted her senses.

'I'm signing some contracts, otherwise I'd have someone else handle things in my place.' He lifted a finger to her cheek, feeling the soft flesh, a smile on his lips as her own parted on a sigh.

She moved her face slightly, so her mouth touched his fingers, and his pupils dilated, passion immediately visible. He pulled his hand away; they both knew what would happen if he didn't.

She loved him. The words were bursting out of her,

as surely as the waves were rolling towards the coast-line. She wanted to say them. She wanted to tell him.

It was this place, she realised, eyes wide. Here, on the island, everything was simple and elemental. They were just a man and a woman, biologically pro-grammed to be together, to want each other, and, for Tessa, to love. The heart she'd sworn would never work again was now working overtime, racing whenever Alex so much as breathed near her.

But the island magnified all those feelings. Here, there were no distractions, no reminders of who she was and the life she had to live. She was running away here, and she couldn't do that any longer.

'I'll come with you,' she said decisively. 'To Athens, I mean.'

He cocked a brow, regarding her thoughtfully. 'It's not necessary. I'll be back before dinner—tomorrow, at the latest.'

Something panged in the region of her heart. For Tessa, the idea of that separation was unbearable, and for him, it rated nothing more than a lift of one shoul-der. Nothing could illustrate their different feelings more than that.

'No.' She couldn't let herself be this woman, so com-pletely in love with him, waiting for him to return. 'I'd like to see my parents, maybe catch up with some friends.' She pushed to standing, finishing her coffee in one gulp. 'I can get ready quickly, okay?'

Her stomach was in knots as his helicopter came in over Athens, the city bleak despite the perfect, golden morning. Landmarks she'd loved all her life, that had fascinated her for their history and culture, now felt like barbed wire against her skin. This was her real life, but she was dreading returning to it. Not because of Jonathan and whatever else he might have said during his time on the show, but because here, in Athens, she knew she would have to put distance between herself and Alex. They wanted this marriage to last, and the only way she could survive a life married to him was to find a way to coexist with the love she felt. That meant returning to the boundaries she'd originally insisted on, and those boundaries would be so much easier to enforce here.

'I'll be done by lunch. Shall we go and see your parents together?'

So much for space and boundaries. 'You could talk to Dad about taking over.'

'You're sure you don't mind?'

She lifted her shoulders. 'It's not up to me.'

Dissatisfaction was obvious in his features. 'None the less, I'd like to know you approved before I suggested it.'

'It will be good for Dad,' she said softly.

'But how do *you* feel about it?'

'Of course I approve. It just seems that you're taking on an awful lot...'

'I can manage.'

Of course he could. He was Alexandros Zacharidis, superman. 'Fine.' Her smile was overbright. 'I'll set it up.'

* * *

It was strange stepping into her parents' house with Alex by her side, and in some ways it felt completely normal. Elizabeth Anastakos pulled her daughter in for a huge hug while Orion and Alex shook hands, and then the older couple shepherded them onto the terrace, where an enormous lunch spreadhad been laid out.

'Mum, you've gone to so much trouble.'

'It was nothing,' Elizabeth said, with her usual humility. Not only did Elizabeth possess a PhD in electrical engineering, but she'd also become her father's right-hand woman, bouncing ideas off one another, and then Stavros. To top it off, she was an exceptional cook, who could make eight dishes without breaking a sweat.

'We could have brought something,' Tessa murmured, old feelings of inadequacy creeping in.

'Next time, we'll come to you,' Orion volleyed back, his skin pale beneath his tan, but his eyes still smiling with pleasure.

We'll come to you. Such a perfectly banal and domestic phrase that spoke of normality and long-term expectations. And could she blame them? It wasn't as if Tessa was planning on leaving Alex. They were married, and at some point they might conceive a child. This was for keeps.

Something tightened in the region of her heart, but she refused to let it unsettle her.

Over lunch, Tessa described Epíneio to them, and whenever she missed a detail Alex was right there to fill in the blanks, answering questions regarding the history of the island house, so she listened in rapt fascination as he spoke. But then, whenever her could hand over to Tessa he did so, deferring to her, allowing her to charm her parents with stories of the beautiful sanctuary.

As they sat back and enjoyed coffee, Tessa too full to ever contemplate eating again, Alex broached the subject of the business.

'I can see a way to alleviate your worries, but, of course, it's a big decision, and one you should weigh up carefully.' He proceeded to outline his proposal, how much he'd pay for a controlling stake in the company—an eye-watering figure—and how he'd juggle his duties across three large multinational companies. 'My father's company and my own run as well-oiled machines. I can step back from both without too much risk, while I come to terms with Anastakos Industries. Naturally, whether or not you're ready to cede control is a personal matter, for you to decide.'

'No, it's not,' Elizabeth demurred, her eyes slightly misty. 'The decision has been made for him.'

Tessa reached over and put a hand on her mother's, stroking it gently.

'You can't keep going on like this, my darling,' Elizabeth said gently to her husband, who harumphed in response. 'And if you're going to see anyone take over, surely it has to be Alex? After Stavros, I wasn't sure he'd ever...'

They were silent, and beneath the table Alex squeezed Tessa's knee comfortingly.

Another noise from Orion, this time one of contemplation.

'Our share values have already gone up at the mere prospect of this,' Orion pointed out.

'That's true. It makes excellent commercial sense.'

'And my wife is right. I'm tired. I would rather be here, with my family, for whatever time I have left.'

Beneath the table, Alex's hand curved over Tessa's knee, as if he understood how desperately she needed that support.

'I can start immediately.'

Relief whooshed through Tessa, on behalf of her father, as well as a strange, aching sense of grief. Alex was talking about undertaking a huge career shift. Superman he might be, and he'd be able to get to the point where her father's company was running as smoothly as his own, but there'd be months, at least, while he learned the ropes and came to terms with the existing commercial arrangements. Months in which he wouldn't be able to fly to Epíneio at the drop of a hat, and she'd be forgotten.

This signalled a shift, surely, in their marriage. After such a short time, the honeymoon was well and truly over.

Lunch stretched into the afternoon, but the sun was still high in the sky as they left, and Tessa, her mind spinning in overtime, couldn't contemplate returning to Alex's home just yet. She needed to make sense of things, to adjust to yet another change in the landscape of their lives.

'Would you mind dropping me at my studio?' she murmured. 'I'd like to work on something. And it would be a good chance to gather some paints for the island,' she added, though who knew when she'd be back?

'Of course,' he replied. 'Address?'

She gave him the street and number, which he keyed into the GPS.

They drove in silence, and the longer it stretched, the more she became aware of a throb of tension between them, until finally, as he pulled up, he turned to face her. 'If you don't want me to buy your family business, just say so.'

Her eyes widened. 'What?'

'You've been mulling since your parents agreed to the sale. So? You're not happy about this after all?'

'I'm very happy for them,' she promised softly, looking at her studio as salvation now. 'You'll do excellent things with it, I'm sure.'

His displeasure was obvious, but she stepped out of the car before he could respond, saying goodbye through the slightly ajar door then closing it and walking quickly away, towards her own Epíneio—the studio.

She leaned against the doors once she'd entered, eyes closed, breathing in deeply.

Everything was going from bad to worse. The boundaries she'd wanted to keep in place were all over the place, and worst of all, her heart couldn't stay out of things. She pushed up from the door and went past her friends' studio spaces to the back, where her own area was, and sat on the stool with a frown on her face, staring at the landscape of Epíneio.

She loved it. Not just the painting, but also the island. It was—

A noise caught her attention and she looked up just as Alex strode in, his features grim. 'You forgot this.' He held up her phone.

She swore softly. Alex's being here was an invasion she hadn't counted on. This was her private space, too intimate for him to see. Too revealing. Anxiously, her eyes shifted to the painting of him, which only served to draw his attention to it, so he followed her gaze and then stood completely still, his expression inscrutable.

'When did you do this?' he asked, eventually, moving closer to the enormous canvas with its striking likeness.

She compressed her lips, the walls closing in on her as the answer seemed likely to give away so much more than she wanted to.

'Tessa?' Sensing it was important, he didn't let her get away with not answering. 'When?'

'After that night,' she said, and he closed his eyes in response.

'I see.' He took another few steps nearer. Her sense of vulnerability increased. 'While you were seeing him?'

She shook her head. 'Does it matter?'

'Why do you have this here?' He moved closer. 'Why do you have a huge painting of me in your studio?' He turned back to it incredulously. 'Why do I look as though I'm laughing at you?'

His words lashed her, but she couldn't help the small simmer of pride at having accomplished what she'd set out to with the work. 'It's just a painting.'

His eyes bored into hers and for a moment she wondered if he was going to pursue this, but then he expelled a sigh and turned his back on it.

'Shall I wait for you?'

'No, no,' she murmured, feigning distraction. 'I could be hours. You go…home.'

He cast the painting one more contemplative glance before leaving.

She added touches to the landscape, but mostly she just stared at it, and remembered. The sunlight on her back, sand underfoot, the simplicity of life on Epíneio, before she'd realised she loved him; again. Still? Making love in the water, on the pool deck, in their bedroom.

A lump formed in her throat. *Their* bedroom. On Epíneio, it really had felt like a shared home, a shared vision.

She worked until the light was gone and then decided she couldn't delay any longer, locking up the studio and moving outside. Just as she was going to hail a cab, she saw headlights across the street and her heart did a funny little patter.

'You waited?' she asked as Alex stepped out of the car.

'I had some calls to make. It was no trouble.'

'Uh-huh.' Just like that, the small shimmy of pleasure faded, because he'd stayed only because it was perfectly convenient for him to do so. *Don't read into it,* was the subtext.

Her stomach squeezed uncomfortably as he came around to the passenger side and opened the door for her. Out of nowhere, she wished this was a motorbike, not a car, and that instead of sliding into a sumptuous leather seat she was curling up behind him, arms wrapped around his waist.

On Epíneio she'd felt unconstrained, the rules of the relationship she'd established out of self-preservation had fallen by the wayside, and she'd allowed herself to feel everything without boundaries, without rules. And Alex? What had he felt?

She frowned, the light seeming to dull a little.

It was obvious that he liked her, and that he respected her. He went out of his way to make her happy. But none of that meant he loved her, nor that he would ever love her, for one simple reason: he didn't want to. And Alex was not a man to feel something he didn't welcome.

She was struck by the irony of buckling her seatbelt. It was protecting her from danger, but what about the danger that came from loving Alex as fiercely as she did? And what choice did she have?

Tessa's pulse fired up a little, as misgivings began to hammer her from the inside out. How in the world could she make this marriage work if she loved him like this, and he didn't feel the same way? And why hadn't she seen this possibility was likely? She'd walked into this marriage so absolutely certain she could control it. What a fool she'd been!

The air simmered with tension as he drove home and expertly parked the car, coming around to her door before she could open it herself.

Once inside, he turned to face her again, his expression impossible to read. Neither spoke for several beats, and then they both did at once.

'Alex—'

'Listen, I—'

She compressed her lips. 'You first.'

He nodded slowly. 'Are you okay?'

'Sure,' she said, overbright. 'Why wouldn't I be?'

'That's what I'm trying to work out. You were fine at your parents'. You say you're happy for me to buy out your father. So what is it?'

How could she explain? How could she tell him the obsessive merry-go-round of thoughts she'd been navigating since realising she loved him? It wasn't fair to put that pressure on him. Nothing had changed since he'd agreed to marry her. She couldn't expect him to love her, just because she wanted him to. He'd made his feelings clear; it wasn't his fault she'd broken their rules.

She lifted a hand to his chest, intending to say something placatory and then move away, but the second her skin connected with his muscled abdomen sparks exploded in her central nervous system.

'Alex,' she sighed, his name a whisper on her lips, a dream and a hope, even when she knew hope was stupid.

In response, he kissed her, hard, as if his frustration at not being able to understand her translated into a frantic need, his dominance overpowering Tessa, so she ran her hands over his body, aching to be close to him, to taste him and feel him.

The same needs were rampant within Alex. He slid his hands inside the waistband of her knickers, brushing his fingers over her sex, finding her flesh and teasing her, before sliding a finger into her moist core so she bucked hard against his hand, aching for more, aching for him. When he touched her like this, nothing else mattered. She felt complete, just in this moment, just for now.

He growled, low in his throat, and their clothes flew, each moving frantically to release them from fabric, to be naked together,

Stars danced in her eyes as his hand returned to her sex, pleasure burst on the tip of her tongue, and then she was exploding, digging her nails into his shoulders as sensations racked her body. Even as the waves were still rolling, not yet receding, he withdrew his hand and lifted her, pushing her back against the wall so he could thrust into her, his arousal filling her, his claim complete, and perfect. She whimpered into the curve of his neck, biting down on her tongue to stop herself from murmuring, over and over like an incantation, the words that were flooding her brain.

I love you. I love you.

But she felt them. Oh, how she felt them, right to the tips of her toes, as he moved within her and she felt the full force of that love. Their coming together was swift, their satisfaction mutual and powerful, their cries mingling as they burst into the heavens together, riding the wave, clinging to one another as though therein lay their only hope of salvation.

But as the waves of pleasure receded for Tessa she wondered if there was no hope of salvation here, but, rather, devastation.

Her first instinct had been to erect boundaries around their lives, to keep Alex at a distance. Had she known, even then, on the day she'd propositioned him, that love might be just as inevitable in this marriage as sex? Was that why she'd wanted to delineate how and when they'd be together?

Of course it was.

And that was no less important now than it had been then.

Unless...

She lifted her face, searching his eyes, looking for some hint of love, needing to know if perhaps he was fighting the same battle she was.

'Tessa?' Concern shaded his eyes.

'I was...' Uncertainty made her pause. If she did this, there'd be no going back. She could swallow these feelings and act as though she didn't have them. She could force them back to the same rigid boundaries she'd implemented in the first place, and act as though that wasn't killing her. But Alex deserved better, and she wanted more.

'You were...?' he prompted, and courage failed Tessa. She needed to talk to him, but it could wait.

'It doesn't matter.' And before he could push the

matter she kissed him again, doing her best not to think about the future, or the complications she'd welcomed by letting her foolish heart fall for him.

CHAPTER THIRTEEN

AS THE NIGHT wore on, the nerves in Tessa's tummy grew tighter, more frantic, so when he went to draw her with him to his bedroom she stood where she was, feet planted on the floor.

On Epíneio, they'd shared a bed every night. There'd been no suggestion of anything else. But here she had her own room, her own space, and if she was to give that up, without knowing how he felt about her, she'd be lost, completely. This emergency marriage that had been entered into as a form of salvation would instead become a silent torment, one from which she could never escape. Because she didn't want to leave Alex. Even loving him as she did, and believing that love to be unrequited, she couldn't turn her back on him. She'd sooner endure the pain of that unreciprocated love than live without him.

'I'm exhausted,' she said with a shake of her head. 'I'm going to my own room.'

He arched his brow with such mocking curiosity that she was reminded immediately of the painting. 'You think I can't be trusted to keep my hands to myself?'

Her heart lurched. 'I think you're as big a risk as I am,' she responded lightly, even though her heart was coiling tighter and tighter.

'I like it when we share a bed. Tell me you don't,' he challenged.

'I do.' She couldn't meet his eyes. 'But it's not really—it doesn't make sense.' Her gut twisted.

'Why not?' His nostrils flared. 'We are married. We were doing it on Epíneio and the world did not end.'

'That's different. The island is different.'

His frown deepened. 'But we are the same people, no?'

She pulled a face. 'Don't be difficult about this, please.'

'Difficult?' he responded, dragging a hand through his hair. 'Two hours ago, we made love as though it was essential for our very survival. Now you are saying you don't want to so much as rest your head on one of my pillows, yet I'm being difficult?'

She nodded slowly. 'That's how it has to be here.' She felt as though she were drowning.

'You're not serious? This again?'

'What?'

'The rules?'

If anything, his derisive response hardened her resolve. 'Nothing's happened to change them.'

'Everything has changed,' he responded, briefly giving her hope. She felt it flare and tried to tamp down on it, but hope was a powerful force and it rolled through her body now.

'Has it?'

'Of course.' He ran his hands through his hair in frustration. 'Look at how much better we know each other, Theresa. When you came to my office and we negotiated that damned contract, you were someone from my past.'

'A mistake,' she interjected with a hint of bitterness.

He ignored that. 'And now you're my wife.' The last word was growled with possession and heat, so her body startled, but she stood still, holding her ground.

'And what does that mean to you?'

His exasperation was obvious. 'That we are married. A team. A *good* team.'

Her heart pounded with nerves. 'That's not enough for me,' she whispered, terrified but knowing her instincts had been wrong: she couldn't put this off, even when she was scared of what he might say. Somehow, knowing he didn't love her would be so much worse than wondering if he did or not, and yet she wanted to have that answer.

'What do you want, then?' he asked, perfectly still, his expression unreadable.

She lifted a finger, toying with the strap of her dress, searching for words. 'I want…' She frowned, still so very anxious. 'I need—'

'Tell me,' he urged, moving closer, the words laced with intensity.

'I want this marriage to be real,' she said finally, eyes lifting to his.

'Did I miss something? Our marriage *is* real.'

That he could think so showed her the truth of his

heart, and yet still she persisted. 'I want us to be a real couple,' she said with quiet determination.

'Again, I feel as though I've missed something. We talk with each other, we eat together, we sleep together. How is this not real?'

She frowned. 'Are you serious?'

'What did you think we were doing, Theresa? On the island there was no one around to witness our behaviour, yet still we touched and kissed and walked along the beach holding hands. That wasn't for the benefit of anyone but you and me. Because we like being that way.'

Liked being that way. 'Yes,' she whispered, 'I did like that.'

His eyes narrowed slightly at her use of a past tense.

'But it's not enough.'

'Then what more do you want?' he asked, as though she could demand a sliver of the moon and he'd find a way to give it to her.

'I want you,' she said simply.

'You have more of me than any woman ever has.'

'I want all of you,' she insisted with a shake of her head. 'I want you to love me, as a husband should love his wife. I want you to wake up in the morning and reach for me not because your body desires mine but because your heart beats for my heart. I want you to kiss me not because you like the way it feels but because your soul has a secret it must share with mine. I want you to be my husband because the idea of being anything else is torture.'

She tilted her face to his, hoping against hope that

he would admit he felt the same way, but he was very still, and very, very silent. As the seconds stretched between them, without him responding, the hope that had started to build inside her dropped as a stone would in water.

'When you suggested this marriage, you were adamant that you'd never love again.'

She closed her eyes, the response not a denial, and yet it may as well have been. 'I remember.'

'You've changed your mind?'

'You changed my mind, actually. I wanted to keep this businesslike, just as we discussed, but every day we spent together was a form of nirvana, and bit by bit I found my way back—to myself, my happiness, my truth, and most importantly to the life I want to lead.'

'Theresa.' He groaned her name. 'This is lust, not love. You were in a deeply unhappy marriage. You've never felt anything like what we share. But sexual infatuation isn't the same thing as love. Nor is friendship. Give it time, you'll see that I'm right.'

His rejection was like a rock, pelting into her belly. Friendship. Sexual infatuation. Was that all this was to him? She took a step back, drawing in a harsh breath. 'You're wrong,' she said, twisting her lips into a tight smile. 'But the fact you can even suggest that tells me how you feel about me.'

'I care about you,' he insisted reflexively. 'You are important to me, and the last thing I want to do is hurt you, but for every part of you that wants our relationship to be real, I know I don't want that. It is everything I have avoided my entire life. I have known, for a long time, that I am someone who values independence. I like the idea of being your husband, of living with you, but as two people on parallel journeys, not entwined in the ways you wish us to be.'

Her heart slowed to an almost-stop. He could not be clearer. Grief tore through her at the finality of his words, suddenly and completely, so much worse than what she'd felt as her marriage to Jonathan had turned dire. That hadn't been soul-destroying because she'd never really loved him. Not like with Alex, who had always threatened to overwhelm her senses.

She lifted a hand to her mouth as she began to understand, only now, why his initial rejection had hurt so much. She'd been terrified. The love that she felt for him was too big, too much; it was a love that could sustain her or destroy her and now she felt the destruction raining down.

Marriage to Jonathan had taught her to conceal her feelings, and she did her best to employ those skills, looking at Alex carefully as she focused on her breathing. Only Alex wasn't Jonathan, and she couldn't keep the turmoil from the shadows of her eyes, nor could she still the breath that was rushing out of her in quick gasps.

'Okay,' she said quietly, the word heavy with her sad acceptance of his stance.

But he moved forward, catching her hands and holding them at chest height. 'Listen, *agape*, this is for your good as much as mine.' His eyes probed hers, as if willing her to understand. 'I cannot be in a marriage like theirs. Love is—a force to be reckoned with, but not

by me. I saw the flipside of it and would never willingly experience that, nor would I put you through it.'
He squeezed her hands.

'But how do you know we'd be like them?' she demanded. 'Look at my parents! They're happy together. Sure, they quarrel sometimes, but they love one another deeply and their lives are better for that.'

'You don't know what it was like,' he said quietly, and sympathy flooded her, because he was right.

'Are you saying you're afraid of loving me?'

His eyes held hers for a long moment, the colour shifting as he contemplated that. 'I won't let it happen.'

'What if it's already happened?'

But he was withdrawing from her. Not physically, emotionally. She could see it in the tightening of his features, the bracing of his shoulders. This was a fight she couldn't win. Childhood had a way of shaping you, sometimes beyond remedy. As a little boy, Alex had seen too much, his heart had felt too deeply, and so he'd closed it down, bit by bit, and there was nothing she could do about that. Not if he didn't dare try.

'You were right in the first place.' He spoke with the appearance of calm. 'Having sex has complicated things unnecessarily. If I had known that sleeping together would make you believe you loved me, I would never have—'

She swore under her breath, interrupting him. 'I don't *believe* I feel it, I do feel it. It's fact, not fiction. And as for *allowing* us to sleep together, I don't think either of us could have stopped it from happening. Just like I couldn't help but love you. Honestly, Alex, I wonder now if I haven't loved you this whole time? That night we slept together it wasn't just physical. Something transformed inside of me, something so big it was terrifying.'

She hesitated, because she'd never planned to tell him this, but now the words came bursting out of her. 'Do you want to know why I did that painting of you?'

Curiosity sparked in his eyes. His nod was deliberate, slow, his gaze intense.

'I couldn't get you out of my head. The things you said to me…' She lifted a hand to her chest and clutched it there, as though she could somehow ease the awful, gutted sensation in her core. 'You destroyed me, Alex.'

'I was—'

But she wasn't ready to be interrupted. 'You broke my heart,' she groaned. 'I loved you then. I'd always loved you. It was easy to think it was just a crush, but now that I know you better, I understand my feelings more. I loved you, and I turned to you when I needed you—not sex, *you*—and you told me it meant nothing, that you wished you could undo what we'd shared. I was devastated. I felt like such an idiot for spending that night with you. And so I painted your face exactly as it had been then, so laced with scorn and disdain, and I made myself look at it every day, to remember never to be such a trusting idiot again.' She swallowed. 'It didn't work though.'

He was very, very still, watching her with a look in her eyes she didn't recognise. 'Did you love me when you married him?'

She dropped her head forward, tears filling her eyes. She'd come this far. 'Yes.'

'So why marry him?' he demanded.

'Why not? You'd made it clear you didn't want me, and I needed to get you out of my damned head somehow.'

He swore under his breath, then pressed his back against the wall, as if needing support. 'All this time,' he said slowly, the words heavy with realisation. 'I've been blaming him for your insecurities, for hurting you, for damaging your confidence. I've been blaming him, but it was me, wasn't it? I'm the one who broke you apart? I'm the one who hurt you.'

A tear fell down her cheek; she dashed it away.

'It was an awful time in my life,' she groaned. 'It's not your fault.'

'Damn it, don't make excuses for me. Don't excuse me. I don't deserve it.'

She flinched.

'Stavros had died, my parents were heartbroken. I wasn't thinking clearly. I needed—'

'A friend,' he groaned, hitting his palm to his forehead. 'At the very least, I owed you that.'

Oh, how much his friendship would have meant to her! 'None of this matters now,' she whispered, throat thick with emotion. 'It changes nothing.'

'It changes *everything*,' he retorted, the words half-yelled. He stared up at the ceiling, his face unreadable. 'You can't love me.'

She felt sympathy for him then, for how even the idea of love was shutting him down.

'Why not?' she demanded, even as a part of her lay dying.

'You can't,' was all he could say. 'Promise me you won't.' It was a demand, not a question. She wanted to deny that, and in her heart she did.

But she loved him enough to prioritise his needs, to understand that he was almost at breaking point.

'I'll stop saying I love you,' she whispered. 'But not feeling it. It's not something that can be turned on and off.' She'd laid it all on the line, but there was no ultimatum, no threat to leave him. Even when there was no hope of his returning her love, she knew she would stay with him, in his orbit, because it was better than living without him. What kind of fool did that make her?

'So now do you understand why I need to sleep in my own room?' she asked, neatly bringing their conversation full circle, and this time he didn't argue. She waited, hoping, even then, but he said nothing, and after a few moments she turned and left, another small tear rolling down her cheek as she stepped from the room.

Over the coming days, Alex realised that there were some things in a marriage that could be worse than his parents' arguing. Silence.

Not companionable silence, but heavy, burdened, painful silence, and smiles that were as fake as the lawn at so many houses. He had felt both from Theresa. He knew the silence was not to punish him, but because there was nothing else they could say.

The easy flow of conversation had disappeared, and

any time he went to speak the words dried in his throat, strangled by his inability to give her the one thing she wanted. As for her smiles…they were an effort. They showed her attempts to keep things even between them, a sign that she wanted to persevere with this marriage even when it fell so wildly short of what she wanted and, hell, what she deserved.

Every moment was agony. He ached for Epíneio. Not just the home, the beach and the breeze, but for how things had been there—so easy and free. He ached to make her laugh, to make her cry with pleasure, to hold her so close he could feel her breath through the walls of his chest. He ached for her.

And yet he kept his distance, because his own needs paled in comparison to hers. He wouldn't hurt her again. Knowing the pain he'd inflicted all those years ago cut him to the core. He'd been such a bastard to her. He couldn't think of it without a deep, mortifying sense of shame. He'd been angry with himself, but he'd lashed out at her. He'd punished her because he'd wanted her so badly. He'd pushed her away, knowing he'd betrayed Stavros and needed her to go, to understand the finality of what he was saying, but he'd destroyed her in the process, and he'd never forgive himself for that. It was remarkable that she had.

As the weekend came around, he thought of their original deal, and the fact she'd agreed Friday through Sunday would be different. He thought about clinging to that lifeline and reimposing those terms, but almost as soon as the idea formed, he dismissed it.

A clean break was better.

If they wanted to salvage their marriage—a marriage that was just a friendship, really—he had to resist temptation. He had to resist Tessa, even when every part of him was yearning for her.

It was the longest month of Tessa's life. Every day she counted off, wondering at what point this would start to get better? She'd always believed in the power of time to heal all wounds, but each day that went by crackled like radio static and, if anything, the pain she felt grew deeper. A week after she'd told Alex she loved him, Tessa had thrown herself into her art. Ten-hour days had stretched to twelve, and then to sixteen. Some nights, she slept on the sofa at the studio rather than go home. She focused all her energy on a large-scale scene, working tirelessly to perfect the details, losing herself in the colours and design.

It helped—barely, but a little. There were even some moments of the day when she was able to put Alex from her mind, but never for long, and the more time she spent estranged from him, the more she craved him. His painting hung across from her, and her eyes flicked to it often, as a talisman, a reminder of what she needed to recover from.

Being home was worse. There, she could feel him. Smell him. See him. It always caught her by surprise, when she'd walk into the kitchen and find him making a coffee, or go to dive into the pool and realise he was already there. For the most part, she would simply turn on her heel and leave the room again, pretending she hadn't realised he was there.

It wasn't because she didn't know what to say to him, but rather that she was scared of pleading her case once more. Of telling him that they could go back to the way they'd been—that she'd never again burden him with her love.

There were many things that led up to it, but in the end it was one thing in particular that made Alex snap. There was the fact that Theresa, always slim and athletic in build, was now far too slender. Her clothes had grown loose and her eyes haunted. Had she realised? Was this on purpose? He knew it wasn't. She simply wasn't eating regularly enough.

She was also working too much. Several nights a week she slept at the studio, though not well, if the bags under her eyes were anything to go by. His own sleep patterns were nothing to boast about. When she didn't come back to their home, he found it hard to sleep—one ear was always trained on the door, listening for her. And when she did come home it was worse, because he lay in bed perfectly aware that they were separated by only a single wall. If he strained, he could hear her when she turned over in her bed, and so he spent a ridiculous amount of time lying there, listening for her movements, and wishing he could reach out and hold her tight.

At least her ex-husband had got the memo and ceased his campaign of misinformation and slander. The lawyers had written a conciliatory response accepting the warning and Alex had reiterated his threats to sue Jonathan to blazes if another word was said about Theresa. At the time, he'd thought the damage Jonathan was doing to her was the devil and he'd done whatever he could to ease her pain. He hadn't realised that he would become a far worse instrument of heart-ache to his wife.

Guilt stormed through him, and something else too: dread.

He had thought this marriage would be the per-fect mix—the exact opposite of what his parents had shared. He had entered into it with a cool head, and yet it had all gone downhill so quickly. Was there any hope they could turn things around? He felt as though they were living in their own war zone, and yet they weren't fighting. They were…nothing. The void of their relationship was almost impossible to accept.

Alex ran a silver fountain pen through his fingers as he contemplated that, his expression grim. A moment later his phone began to ring—it was Tessa.

'Theresa?'

'Um, is this Alex?' An American voice reached his ears, and a trickle of dread ran down his spine.

'Yes. Who is this?'

'My name's Beth. I work at the studio, with Tess.' His eyes swept shut as instinctively he felt something change in the air around him.

'Yes?' The word was clipped.

'She passed out. She didn't want me to call you, she says she's fine now, but she's pale and I thought—'

He gripped the phone tighter, standing. 'I'll be there immediately. I'm calling a doctor—she might get there before me.'

'She seems okay now,' Beth murmured, clearly not expecting this whirlwind response. 'I don't know if she needs—'

'I want a doctor to see her to be sure. I'll be there soon.'

He was already in the lift, and as soon as the doors pinged open on the ground floor he began to run to his car. Suddenly, the idea of there being any distance between them was like eating fire. He couldn't stand it. He needed to be with her, and to hell with overthinking that. To hell with everything.

CHAPTER FOURTEEN

'I TOLD YOU, I'm fine,' Tessa muttered, considerably *less* fine now than she had been a moment earlier, before Alex had burst into the studio, midway through the doctor he'd sent drawing blood from the crook of her arm.

'Doctor?' Alex turned his attention to the middle-aged woman with the reassuring bearing. 'What's going on? How is she?'

'Dehydrated,' the doctor replied without lifting her gaze, removing the needle and pressing a cotton ball against the skin, stemming the blood droplet. 'Beyond that, I won't know until I get these results.' She lifted the three vials of blood and then slipped them into the pocket of her lab coat, only then making eye contact with Alex.

'But you suspect something is wrong?' Alex demanded, not looking in Tessa's direction, so she had a moment to stare at him, and she took it, drinking in the sight of him while he was distracted, allowing herself to commit every detail to memory. It had been weeks since she'd properly looked at him, longer since they'd touched. Her heart did a funny little palpating thing and she let out a soft groan.

Alex turned to her at once, then crouched beside her. '*Agape,* what is it?'

If she'd thought that term of endearment hard to hear before, it was nothing compared to now that she had confirmation he didn't love her. She offered him a tight smile, hoping it was reassuring. 'I'm just—I'm fine,' she said, her eyes skittling away from him and towards the doctor, who nodded professionally.

'I should have these results by tomorrow.'

'Tomorrow?' Alex stood, turning to face the doctor, his shoulders squared. 'That's too long. Send them to a different lab, I don't care what it costs.'

The doctor's expression was one of patience, as though she'd heard that before. 'I will put a rush on them,' she said politely, then turned to face Tessa, 'and call you when I have the results.'

Tessa nodded her thanks and went to stand, to accompany the doctor to the door, but her legs were still wobbly and she swayed a little, so Alex rushed to her, placing a strong, commanding arm around her waist, holding her against his side. Little electric shocks flooded her. It felt so good to be touched by him, to be felt by him, she just wanted to stay there a little longer, to take strength from him.

'I'll speak to you soon, Mrs Zacharidis.'

Beth, standing by and watching, eyed the couple. 'Do you want a coffee, Tess? A muffin?'

Tessa didn't feel like anything, but she nodded, because she felt as though Alex was about to explode.

When they were alone she went to pull away from him, but he held her tight, right where she was, staring down at her thoughtfully for several seconds, before swinging her into his arms and carrying her, cradled against his chest, from the studio.

'What are you doing?' she demanded, looking around despite the fact they were alone.

'Fixing this,' he said through gritted teeth.

Even though it was cheating, she let her head rest on his shoulder, and she listened to the beating of his heart, the proximity giving her the strength she needed. But when he stepped out of the building and approached his car, she knew she had to assert her independence once more.

'Alex, I'm serious, what do you think you're doing?'

'I told you, fixing—'

'Nothing needs fixing,' she denied. 'Beth will—'

'I will call her and explain,' he insisted as he opened the front passenger door to his car, helping Tessa in. She was too exhausted to struggle. He came around to the driver's side quickly and looked at her as though reassuring himself of something, then started the engine with a dramatic roar and pulled out into traffic.

It took several blocks before Tessa realised they weren't moving towards his home, and several more minutes to recognise where they were going. Her insides clenched as his helicopter came into view, and suspicion began to form.

'No.' She shook her head, the idea of being back on Epíneio a torture she couldn't withstand. After all, the island was where she'd realised she loved him, that she'd always loved him.

'Yes,' he muttered, killing the engine and coming around to her door. When she didn't move, he unbuckled her seatbelt then lifted her from the car, carrying her once more towards the helicopter.

'Damn it, Alex, I can walk, I'm fine.'

'Just let me do this, for God's sake.'

She startled, the tone of his voice pulling at something in her heart. She hesitated a moment and then nodded. Epíneio scared her but there was something about Alex that worried her more than she was scared, something about him that seemed…shattered.

'Thank you.' The words were dredged from the depths of his soul. Only once they reached the helicopter did he set her down, holding her hand to help her up then coming around to the pilot's side and taking his own seat. She buckled in while he adjusted the controls and started the rotor blades spinning, then they were up, Athens shrinking into a model city before her eyes.

From time to time, Tessa was afflicted by travel sickness and her exhaustion translated into nausea, so as Alex expertly piloted the chopper towards Epíneio, she pressed her head against the headrest and closed her eyes, dozing in the streaming sunlight until he set the helicopter down and gently tapped her knee, waking her. She looked at him, nothing making sense for a moment, and then she sat up straighter, her heart bolting as she saw the island.

Somehow, the place was even more beautiful now.

Her heart twisted and yearned for something that was impossible.

Tears threatened and she dug her nails into her palms to stave them off, but when Alex came around to her side, she suspected he knew how she felt, because his jaw tightened and his face bore a mask of concern.

'I'm fine,' she reassured him. 'Please, stop worrying.'

His response was to take her hand and help her down from the helicopter, but before he could lift her again she shook her head. 'I'm okay to walk. Please, Alex, don't fuss. I just fainted a moment, it was nothing really.'

'It's not…it's not just that you passed out,' he said, shaking his head, silencing whatever else he'd been about to say. He tugged on her hand lightly. 'Come inside.'

She nodded, but with each step that brought them closer to the house she felt as though a piece of her was breaking off, so before they reached the delightful doors she stopped walking and stood completely still, staring at it. 'I don't know if I can do this,' she said, the words strained.

'Oh?'

She threw a quick glance at him, reminding herself she'd said she would never burden him with her love again. He'd been honest about his feelings all along, it wasn't his fault she'd broken the terms of their arrangement.

'It's complicated,' she said finally, the words halting.

'Is it? To me, it seems very simple. Here, we were happy. And I have not been happy since. Have you?'

She almost rolled her eyes. 'This isn't real life, though. We were happy here because it was a holiday. No, a fantasy.'

'Was it? Was loving me also a fantasy?'

Her heart squealed but her mind flicked to life. Perhaps that was a way to let him off the hook? She could lie to him and say that yes, everything she'd felt had been a fantasy, none of it was real. But she *couldn't* lie to him. Not about something so important.

'What I wanted was an illusion,' she said carefully, eyes roaming the house now, frown on her lips. She was unaware of the way Alex stared at her, nor of the way his own mouth turned downwards.

'Then come inside to rest for a time. Eat. Drink. Swim. You have been working too hard.'

'I love my work.'

'And it will still be waiting for you, or you can use the studio here.'

'How would you feel if I ripped you out of your office?'

'If I looked as dead on my feet as you do, relieved,' he muttered, throwing her a warning glance. 'Do I need to carry you the rest of the way?'

She was here now—the only alternative to going into the house was insisting he fly her back to Athens, and that filled her with a bag of cement. 'Fine,' she agreed mutinously. 'I'll go inside.'

But it was like stepping back into the past. The last time they'd left, they'd both presumed they'd come

back again soon after, and the house had that feeling—
as though it had been left quickly, everything still exactly as it was. Her heart turned over in her chest as
she walked deeper into the living room, her pulse going
wild as memories flooded her.

'You were happy here,' he said quietly, moving to
stand behind her. 'I like seeing you happy.'

Her eyes swept shut, because she heard what he
wasn't saying. He didn't like seeing her hurt. He didn't
like knowing he'd hurt her. He was terrified of turning
into his father and worried their marriage was going to
dissolve into that same awful merry-go-round of fights.

She turned to face him, needing to reassure him.
'I'm happy in Athens too,' she lied.

'You're avoiding me,' he said flatly. 'You hide from
me at home. You leave any room I am in. We have not
had a conversation in over a month. Do you want a divorce, *agape*? Because I would accept that—I would
accept anything—rather than seeing you like this and
knowing me to be the cause.'

Her pulse hit a crescendo and her eyes stung with
unshed tears. 'Do *you* want a divorce?' She volleyed
the question back to him.

Alex's eyes flared to hers, something deep in their
irises. She held her breath, waiting, her nerves stretching to breaking point. Finally, he shook his head. 'That
is the opposite of what I want.'

She exhaled slowly, nodding. 'It would be bad for
my father.'

His eyes were shielded from her by his long lashes.
'That's true.'

Had she been hoping for a denial? Her heart thumped. 'I'm sorry if what I told you the other week made things difficult for you,' she said quietly. 'It won't happen again.'

'Don't.' His voice rumbled towards her. 'Don't apologise. Your love was a gift. That you wanted to share that with me will always be meaningful.' He paused, drawing in a deep breath so his chest lifted and fell. 'I haven't been honest with you, *agape*.'

She flinched at the term of endearment.

'Do you remember the art show you had in Florence? Around your twenty-first birthday.'

Of course she did. It was only her second show, the first having garnered so much praise she'd been given a huge venue just down a lane from the Uffizi, at one of the most prestigious private galleries in Europe. 'What about it?'

'Stav was so proud of you. He spoke of nothing else for days.' He angled his face away, staring at the wall. 'I said nothing to him. Nothing that would lead him to think I'd been thinking about it, and you. Nothing to make him wonder.'

'I don't understand.'

'And then, I went to the gallery. I flew there especially, telling myself I was simply curious, that my interest was natural. But why didn't I tell Stav? Why didn't I go with him?' His voice was laced with self-condemnation. 'On some level, I knew that my feelings were wrong. They were so much deeper than I could ever admit to. I went, I saw, I was blown away by your talent, and then I left, and told no one.' His eyes bored into hers with fierce intensity. 'You are so clever. Gifted. And then you stopped.'

She turned away from him, his words chewing through her resolve and causing hope to flicker to life—but hadn't she told herself hope was a wasted force?

'I was terrified,' he admitted gruffly, his words spoken to her back. 'I have been so determined to avoid love, all my life, and very specifically to avoid loving you. For as long as I've known you, there's been something between us, something I've fought to resist.' She closed her eyes on a wave of pain. 'To have you offer it to me so bravely, so beautifully, even after what I've put you through, was overwhelming. On so many levels, this is wrong—I have told myself this is wrong, that I couldn't have you.'

She let out a small cry of hopelessness, for the pain he'd put them both through.

'I wanted to avoid hurting you, with all that I am. I wanted to avoid hurting you as my father hurt my mother, and then I had to watch you disappear from me, fade away into nothing, your face pale, your eyes haunted, and I have known it is my fault. Everything I dreaded most came to pass regardless of how I tried to avoid it.' He dropped his head forward, rubbing the back of his neck. 'I was so angry at myself, Theresa. Whenever I replayed that conversation and heard what I said to you, I wanted to shake myself. Why couldn't I admit to you that I was scared of the love you were offering?'

She made a gargling sound, moving now to the sofa

and sitting down. The support was a godsend. 'I knew you felt that. You didn't need to say anything.'

He crossed to her and knelt at her feet, just as he'd done in her studio. 'But since then I have felt a thousand things, and none of them made any sense until today. I could not understand why my chest was hurting and my mind was singularly obsessed with you—where you were, what you were doing, how you were feeling. Memories of Epíneio, of your smile, your laugh, of being here together, tormented me at all hours of the day and still I didn't understand. I knew only that I'd had something special and lost it. That I'd lost you. Suddenly, I was going through the motions of life without feeling that I was actually living.'

Her eyes stayed on her knees; it was impossible to look at him.

'And then today, when your friend called and told me you'd passed out, I had no idea what had happened, or how serious it was. But in that moment I would have struck any bargain with any god for you to be okay. I couldn't face the prospect of living without you, *agape,* because no matter how hard I have tried to fight it, I love you, as absolutely as the stars are a part of the sky, I love you. Is it possible I always have?'

She made an uneven sound as the words burst around them, and she lifted a hand to his shoulder. She wanted to feel euphoria, but doubts plagued her. 'Please don't feel you have to say this. I really am okay, Alex. I'm not dying. I'm not even sick. I've just been pushing myself a bit too hard. If this is guilt or some weird sense of responsibility talking, then shelve it.

I'll be fine.' She jutted her chin defiantly, desperately needing him to understand. 'I'm not your mother, and you're not your father.'

'No. We're our own people, with our own lives to lead. I get that now. There is no one kind of marriage, no one kind of love.' He leaned closer, his thumb catching her hair and pushing it behind one ear. 'And I know you will be fine, my darling, but I won't be. I have been miserable since that night, and only today have I properly understood the reason.' His eyes scanned hers, truth in his face. 'I love you. Just as you said, this is not a sudden love, it is a love I think I have felt for a long time. The night of the funeral, when we came together, it wasn't just grief. It was because I needed to make love to you, the only person on earth who had the power to make me feel better—the person who has been, for a long time, my other half.'

Her eyes parted. 'The way you reacted—'

'I was terrified,' he said quietly. 'When I was with you, I felt whole. I felt better. Like the best version of myself. One night with you and I felt everything I'd always believed torn away from me, violently, and I wasn't ready.'

She shook her head, eyes sweeping shut. 'You were so final.'

He paused, obviously weighing up his next words with care.

'There's something else, something I should have told you sooner.'

She held her breath, bracing herself for whatever was coming next.

'Your brother was very protective of you.'

She expelled a cross sigh. 'We've discussed that.'

But Alex continued as though she hadn't spoken. 'He knew you had a crush on me, and if he caught me so much as looking in your direction he would warn me away. He would joke about it, but we both knew he meant every word. I was older, too experienced, not right for you. To have slept with you right after we buried him…can you understand how I felt? I was so ashamed of myself, so angry that I'd betrayed Stavros in that way, and I lashed out. It was wrong, and it was far from an accurate representation of my feelings. I pushed you away, but not because I didn't care about you. That was never why.'

Her eyes sparkled with tears.

'I love you,' he added, simply, when all more grandiose forms of expression seemed unnecessary. 'And I am going to keep you here until you understand that.'

She laughed. 'I think I understand already,' she blinked her lashes, 'but I'm happy to pretend I don't, just for tonight.'

'A few nights,' he bartered, then, before she could demur, he lifted a finger to her lips, silencing her. 'At least.'

She nodded, her heart bursting. 'That sounds like heaven to me.'

Much later, with their feet in the balmy water of the Aegean, the sky dusky pink and orange, Tessa's phone began to ring. She lifted it from her back pocket, frowning at the unfamiliar number, then swiped to answer.

'Hello?'

'Is this Theresa Zacharidis?'

She smiled up at Alex, her heart full to the brim, because she really *was* Theresa Zacharidis, in every bone of her body, and all the cells of her heart. 'Yes indeed.'

'It's Dr Baros.'

'Oh, hello, Doctor,' she smiled, having forgotten all about the incident in her studio that morning. Truly, it felt like a lifetime ago.

'I've just seen the results of your blood tests—'

'And everything's fine?' Tessa pre-empted.

'Well, yes…' The doctor hesitated. 'Only, I think I've discovered the reason you fainted.'

'I've been pushing myself too hard,' Tessa supplied.

'Perhaps, but that's not the sole reason.'

'It's not?' She wrinkled her brows, ignoring Alex's concerned expression. Then, to placate him, she put it on speaker. 'Doctor? Alex is here too. I've put you on loudspeaker.'

'And you're happy for him to hear this?'

She looked at Alex, nodding. Whatever concerned her, concerned him too. They were partners, a pair. That was how it would always be. 'Yes.'

'Then congratulations. You're pregnant, Theresa.'

Tessa's knees wobbled beneath her, and Alex made a strange sound, his eyes shining, and then he smiled, the biggest, most genuine smile she'd ever seen, so there was no doubt in her mind as to how this news affected him. For her part, it was as though lightning bolts were firing all through her body. She was coming alive in a way that made her feel that her seams might burst.

'Pregnant,' she repeated, shaking her head in wonder.

'I take it this is a surprise?'

'You could say that.'

'Have you had any other symptoms?'

'Well, the thought of food has made me feel absolutely nauseated for about six weeks.'

The doctor laughed. 'That explains it.'

'I can't believe it.' Tessa shook her head, smiling from ear to ear.

'You can come and see me tomorrow, to go through the prenatal information...'

'I'm not in Athens right now,' Tessa murmured, squeezing Alex's hand.

'We will come back immediately,' he interrupted.

'It's not urgent.' The doctor's smile could be heard through the phone. 'Everything looks fine. Your blood tests show as great, in fact. Iron, Vitamin D, everything looks to be perfect. Only try to find something you can stomach the idea of eating—for the baby's sake.'

'I will.' Tessa nodded.

'And book an appointment some time in the next fortnight. We'll do a scan and go over things in more detail.'

'Doctor? Can you tell how far along I am?'

'It's difficult to say without doing a scan, but going from the level of hormones in your blood I'd say around six weeks.'

Tessa thought her heart might burst. 'That makes sense,' she smiled serenely, disconnecting the call a moment later and looking up at Alex.

'Does it?' he repeated, with wonder.

'I think it happened on our last night here, in the pool. It was when I knew, without a shadow of a doubt, how much I loved you.'

He tilted his head back and laughed, then wrapped his arms around her waist and lifted her into the air, spinning her around then slowly sliding her down his body, kissing her when their faces were level. 'You had no idea?'

'None,' she promised. 'I've been so distracted…'

'And at least I know now that your food aversion wasn't sparked by my awful behaviour.'

She shook her head, not wanting to tell him how hard his rejection had hurt. She leaned closer, lifting up onto her tiptoes to kiss him, as everything in her world clicked into place.

'I love you,' he said, and they were the three most beautiful words in the world, because they were true and right and always would be. She held him tight and loved him back, with all her heart, her soul, and every single piece of her, for all time.

EPILOGUE

SECOND CHANCES IN life were a gift, not a guarantee, and Alex and Tessa knew that deep in their bones. They'd been given a second chance and neither was willing to waste a moment of it.

Epíneio became not just a haven but also a home, a place for family to gather and celebrate, to be together, to make loud, happy memories, and also to remember. Stavros was spoken of so often that he felt very much a part of their lives, and when his namesake was born, eight months after Alex and Tessa recommitted to one another on Epíneio, it was with the certainty that little baby Stavros would always know about his uncle.

Orion and Elizabeth visited as often as his health would allow, and when he became too weak to travel to the island, Tessa, Alex and baby Stavros visited his home in Athens. He lived to see Stavros turn one, and Tessa's belly grow round with their second baby, to witness her first art showing in years, to marvel at her talent, and to recognise her finally, fully, as the woman she'd always been destined to become.

When Orion died there was grief and sadness, and

so much heartache, but there was also hope and joy, because his life had been long and lived with meaning, and just as they honoured Stavros, they honoured Orion, and kept his memories with them always.

A cottage was built for Elizabeth on Epíneio, and after the birth of their fifth child Alex and Tessa were ever grateful to have a doting grandmother on hand to help care for their children, and to allow them the freedom to occasionally travel as a couple. For as much as they loved their children—and they did, with all their hearts—their family of seven had begun as two, and the love of that pair was something special and beautiful that each wanted to celebrate, whenever they could.

There was no contract that could contain their love, no term or agreement that could bind them more than the agreement their hearts had made, secretly, quietly, a long, long time ago.

Alexandros Zacharidis was not a man to make mistakes, and as it turned out he hadn't.

* * * * *

If you didn't want to put
Emergency Marriage to the Greek *down,*
then why not lose yourself in these other
Clare Connelly stories?

My Forbidden Royal Fling
Crowned for His Desert Twins
Vows on the Virgin's Terms
Forbidden Nights in Barcelona
Cinderella in the Billionaire's Castle

Available now!

WE HOPE YOU ENJOYED
THIS BOOK FROM

⟨H⟩ HARLEQUIN

PRESENTS

Escape to exotic locations where passion knows no bounds.

Welcome to the glamorous lives of royals and billionaires, where passion knows no bounds. Be swept into a world of luxury, wealth and exotic locations.

8 NEW BOOKS AVAILABLE EVERY MONTH!

#4041 THE KING'S CHRISTMAS HEIR
The Stefanos Legacy
by Lynne Graham

When Lara rescued Gaetano from a blizzard, she never imagined she'd say "I do" to the man with no memory. Or, when the revelation that he's actually a future king rips their passionate marriage apart, that she'd be expecting a precious secret!

#4042 CINDERELLA'S SECRET BABY
Four Weddings and a Baby
by Dani Collins

Innocent Amelia's encounter with Hunter was unforgettable... and had life-changing consequences! After learning Hunter was engaged, she vowed to raise their daughter alone. But now, Amelia's secret is suddenly, scandalously exposed!

#4043 CLAIMED BY HER GREEK BOSS
by Kim Lawrence

Playboy CEO Ezio will do anything to save the deal of a lifetime. Even persuade his prim personal assistant, Matilda, to take a six-month assignment in Greece...as his convenient bride!

#4044 PREGNANT INNOCENT BEHIND THE VEIL
Scandalous Royal Weddings
by Michelle Smart

Her whole life, Princess Alessia has put the royal family first, until the night she let her desire for Gabriel reign supreme. Now she's pregnant! And to avoid a scandal, that duty demands a hasty royal wedding...

HPCNMRA0822

#4045 THEIR DESERT NIGHT OF SCANDAL
Brothers of the Desert
by Maya Blake

Twenty-four hours in the desert with Sheikh Tahir is more than Lauren bargained for when she came to ask for his help. Yet their inescapable intimacy empowers Lauren to lay bare the scandalous truth of their shared past—and her still-burning desire for Tahir...

#4046 AWAKENED BY THE WILD BILLIONAIRE
by Bella Mason

Colliding with a masked stranger at a ball sends shy Emma's pulse skyrocketing. And that's *before* he introduces himself as Alexander Hastings, the CEO with a wild side, which puts him way out of her league! Will Emma step out of the shadows and into the billionaire's penthouse?

#4047 THE MARRIAGE THAT MADE HER QUEEN
Behind the Palace Doors...
by Kali Anthony

To claim her crown, queen-to-be Lise must wed. The man she must turn to is Rafe, the self-made billionaire who once made her believe in love. He'll have to make her believe in it again for passion to be part of their future...

#4048 STRANDED WITH HIS RUNAWAY BRIDE
by Julieanne Howells

Surrendering her power to a man is unacceptable to Princess Violetta. Even *if* that man sets her alight with a single glance! But when Prince Leo tracks his runaway bride down and they are stranded together, he's not the enemy she first thought...

YOU CAN FIND MORE INFORMATION ON UPCOMING HARLEQUIN TITLES, FREE EXCERPTS AND MORE AT HARLEQUIN.COM.

HPCNMRB0822

"Emma," Alex said, pinning her against the wall in a spectacularly graffitied alley, the walls an ever-changing work of art, when he could bear it no more. "I have to tell you. I really don't care about seeing the city. I just want to get you back in my bed."

He could barely believe that he wanted to take her back home. Sending her on her way was the smarter plan. But how smart was it really to deny himself? Emma knew the score. This wasn't about feelings or a relationship. It was just sex.

"Give me the weekend. I promise you won't regret it." His voice was low and rough. He could see in her eyes